BURNING LIES (SPECIAL FORCES: OPERATION ALPHA)

AIR FORCE FIRE PROTECTION SPECIALISTS BOOK 4

JEN TALTY

To Susan Stoker. Thank you for inviting me into such an amazing world. You are an inspiration to us all.

And to Casey Hagen. Thank you for answering the phone each and every time I call. You are my writing rock.

BLURB

Air Force Senior Fire Protect Specialist, Brayden "Brodie" Welch is at the height of his career and up for a promotion. He knows he's going to get it until the unthinkable happens.

A fire on base takes the life of one of their own and Brodie becomes the center of the investigation.

When Air Force Investigation Officer Harper Dawson first meets Brodie Welch she sees him as the sexy as hell, but clean-cut boy next door type. That is until his missing gas can is found at the fire that took the life of a fellow Air Force fireman. Now Harper finds herself having to arrest the man she's falling in love with.

Harper doesn't want to believe, but the evidence against Brodie is too damaging to ignore.

However, when the investigation takes a dark and

dangerous twist, Harper finds herself relying on Brodie. Together, in the burning ruble, they uncover lies so devastating it will change the direction of their lives.

CHAPTER 1

"Wake up. Your birthday is over."

Brodie Welch groaned as he rolled to his side, pulling the covers over his head, ignoring his roommate and fellow Air Force Fire Protection Specialist, Declan Rivers.

"Bug off," Brodie managed to say even though his lips stuck together like dried cotton.

"It's your turn to mow the lawn," Declan said with a sarcastic laugh.

"What are you, my wife?" Brodie had moved in six months ago when Declan's long-time girlfriend moved out and moved on, leaving Declan with a broken heart. Even if he acted like the break up was no big deal, Brodie knew better. He and Declan had gone through the Air Force Academy and Fireman

Training together and Declan was more like a brother than a friend.

"No woman on the planet would have you, especially in this condition. You look like shit."

Brodie glanced at his knuckles and then cupped his bruised cheek. He hadn't gotten into a fist fight since high school, so at thirty-four, he was more than out of practice, but that asshole, Jonathon Battle deserved a good punch. Not just for his rude comments to the newest member of his team, but in general, he was a cocky son-of-a-bitch and certainly not a team player. The few times Brodie had to work a fire with Jonathon, he hadn't felt safe and that meant people could die. Firemen had to put their lives in the hands of the man standing next to him and be responsible in return. Something that didn't happen with Jonathon.

Currently, Jonathon had been moved to a desk position for thirty days because he'd failed to follow protocol, the mind-numbing monotony just making him more of a dick.

"I feel like death." Brodie sat up, resting his back on the headboard and stared at Declan, who stood in the bedroom doorway looking like the front cover of the latest Fireman and Puppies calendar. Brodie's memory might be a little fuzzy from last night's celebration, but he knew Declan had tossed back more than a few. "I'm getting too old for this shit."

"I'm sure Jonathon's face looks worse than yours."

"I hope he gets transferred, but I don't wish that asshole on anyone." Brodie rubbed his forehead, but he knew the only thing that would cure his hangover was a greasy bacon cheeseburger with a fried egg and a gallon of water. "How are you not hung-over?" Brodie asked.

"Oh, trust me, I am. I made love to the porcelain God for a good half hour early this morning. I forced myself to take a hot shower and then I went and got us breakfast."

"You are the fucking man," Brodie said, pushing back the covers as he found his shorts. His feet hit the floor, and his vision tripled. A wave of nausea rolled from his fuzzy brain to his sloshy gut. He pressed his hands against the wall to steady himself. "I used to be able to handle my liquor."

"At least you didn't trip and land face-first in the cake," Declan said, shaking his head.

"Poor girl." One of the last things Brodie remembered was helping the newest member of their team, Becca Knowles, back to her rental four blocks away on Avocado Street in the quaint neighborhood of

Satellite Beach. He'd tucked her into her bed and stumbled back to his house with a bottle of Jack Daniels that Becca had told him to take because she never wanted to see it again.

And she was a whopping twenty-five years old, so one might think she could party like a rock star.

"We should go check on her." Brodie blinked a few times as he stepped into his shorts, hiking them up over his hips.

"I already did. She's headed out for a run. Asked if we wanted to join her."

"To be young again." Brodie slapped Declan on the shoulder as he pushed past him, heading toward the kitchen. The three-bedroom ranch they leased from a wealthy family who had at least a half-dozen houses in the neighborhood that had all been leased to military personnel. His people. "Do we have coffee?"

"I'm not your wife, remember? But I made a pot."

"Thank God for small favors," Brodie mumbled, scratching his head, the cobwebs starting to fade into the distance. The smell of bacon and meat filled his nostrils, easing his sour belly. "I'm starving." After getting a mug and filling it, he sat at the table and pulled open the to-go container, his stomach turning over with one big growl.

"What do you think of Becca?" Declan asked.

That got Brodie's attention. Declan had been on an anti-woman campaign for months, saying he'd never get involved again. But Declan was a one-woman man, and everyone knew it. He just had shit taste in the ladies.

"I think she's smart and a great addition to our team," Brodie said.

"I know a few teams who are glad they didn't get assigned a female."

"And they are all sexist assholes. Women make for some great first responders." For years, Brodie had to help his twin sister, Madison, fight for what she wanted and now she was a Deputy Chief Fireman in their hometown in Vermont, but she still had to deal with the misconception that being a woman meant she couldn't save lives and fight fires. "But that's not why you're asking, now is it?"

"She flirted with me last night," Declan said as if that were a horrible thing.

"I know. She wanted you to walk her home, but you were nowhere to be found."

"Truth be told, I was hiding from her."

Brodie lifted the burger and took the largest bite he could stuff in his face. Whoever created hang-over food should be given the Pulitzer or something.

He closed his eyes, enjoying the way the grease rolled down his throat. The bacon crunched between his teeth, and the fried egg exploded like a mini orgasm in his mouth.

He nearly choked at the off-color thought.

"Why the hell would you do that?" Brodie asked before taking another bite.

"I think she's pretty damn incredible, but so fucking young, and I work with her. What the hell am I doing even thinking about it?" Declan shoved a French fry into his mouth. "Besides, I listened to her talk about the last guy she was involved with, and I'm not sure I want to walk into that mess."

"Not to sound like your future Crew Chief, but it's never a good idea to be involved with someone you work side by side with."

"I can't believe you got Ace's job." Declan had always been good at taking the first opening in changing the subject. If he wanted to talk more about Becca, he would.

"I can't believe Ace is going to be Department Captain. Hard for me to picture him in a desk job." For as long as Brodie had been stationed at Patrick Air Force Base, Ace had been his Crew Chief.

"I think with his wife pregnant with their third

kid, he's feeling his mortality," Declan said, diverting his gaze to the ceiling.

Brodie knew without a shadow of a doubt, Declan wanted a wife, kids, and the white picket fence.

Hell, so did Brodie, but he'd yet to find a woman that took his breath away and made him want to do something crazy like 'put a ring on it.' So, until that day happened, if it ever did, he'd enjoying being a bachelor.

Though, he would do his best to avoid a hang-over from now on.

"I better go mow the lawn before my roommate has a cow." Brodie downed two large gulps of coffee, thankful it wasn't scalding hot. Grabbing the rest of his burger, he headed toward the back door and paused. "Thanks for a great birthday, man."

"Anytime."

Brodie stepped into the garage and hit the clicker. The warm sun filtered through the opening. With hurricane season behind them, the tempera-tures had started to drop, but that didn't seem to stop the lush green growth of the grass yet. He pushed the lawnmower out to the driveway, noting a white SUV parked at the house across the street and one door down with the hatch open. That place had been empty for the last two months since it sold. Someone told him that the new owner wouldn't be renting it out, but moving in. Only no one had moved in yet.

Bending over, still staring at the house, he snatched the cord just as a woman in a pair of white shorts, showing off tanned legs that went on forever, graced his vision Her black tank top hugged her mid-drift and breasts, showing off her tight abs and her curvy top. Her dark hair flowed over her shoulders. She peered over her large-rimmed sunglasses and waved. Her smile socked him in the chest.

He pulled the rip cord on the mower with manly gusto, ready to show her his awesome stud status but instead, he yanked in an awkward direction and fell over backward.

"Fuck," he said with a moan as he landed on his ass on the concrete driveway.

"You okay?" the woman asked as she raced across the street.

"I'm fine." Only his bruised male ego took a major hit.

The woman stood over him, holding out her hand. "So, you're Air Force Fire Protection."

"How'd you know?" he asked as his lungs deflated. He tried to suck in another breath, but it seemed for the first time in his life—a woman stole it.

She tapped her chest, right above her damn perfectly round womanly curves. "I recognize the tatt."

He'd forgotten he was in only his shorts. Taking her hand, he jumped to his feet, only he didn't allow her to help. He just wanted to touch her skin.

His pulse raced with the kind of adrenaline rush he had right before he ran into a burning building.

"Are you moving in?" Brodie asked, still holding onto her hand and staring into her almond-mocha eyes.

She nodded. "I'm Harper Dawson."

"Brodie Welch."

"It's nice to meet you," she said, pulling her hand away. "I've got to get going. I need to get a few things before the moving truck gets here. I hope to see you soon."

"Maybe tonight we can have a drink. Yeah. Stop by. Me and my roommate, Declan, will just be hanging out. Might as well come over for dinner. I mean, who wants to cook while they still have to unpack?" Jesus, he sounded like a fucking moron as he babbled on and stumbled over his words.

"I have a meeting I have to attend around five, so maybe a drink later on."

"Hope to see you then."

She nodded, slipping her large sunglasses back on her face. Her hips swayed as she crossed the street.

Brodie tore his gaze away as he turned his attention back to the lawn mower. Jerking the cord, this time without falling over, the engine turned over once, then puttered out. He tried two more times before he realized the damn thing was out of gas.

He snatched the gas can from the garage and put it in the back of his pickup before heading back into the house to snag his keys and a shirt.

Declan still sat at the kitchen table, sipping coffee and scarfing down fries.

"We need gas," Brodie said, pointing at the back door that just slammed shut. "And I met our new neighbor. She's stopping by for a drink tonight. For me, not you, so don't embarrass me or hit on her."

Declan laughed. "Because falling on your ass didn't shame you enough?"

Brodie rubbed his bruised ass and winced at the thought. "I'm going to go get—"

The cell phone on the table buzzed as the song *Maggie May* belted from the small electronic device.

"It's Ace," Declan tapped the phone, sending it to speaker. "What's up, boss?"

"How are you feeling this morning?" Ace asked. He'd left the party long before it had gotten out of hand. Smart man.

"I'm not dead."

"Where's Brodie?"

"Right here, boss," Brodie said.

"I hate to ask since you both haven't had a few days off in a long time, but it's been abnormally busy out there, and we need coverage for a local station."

Brodie had never said no to helping out, and he wouldn't start now. "I can be there in twenty."

"I'll come in with Brodie," Declan said.

"It's an overnight shift," Ace said.

"Not a problem, boss," Brodie said. In three weeks, he'd be Crew Chief, and while that would change his role on the team, it wouldn't change the crazy hours, or the men and women he had the honor of working with.

And that was just fine with him.

CHAPTER 2

Harper sat on the front step of her new home feeling a sense of pride that only ownership could bring, but even that couldn't change that today was the anniversary of the single most painful event in her life.

She glanced at her phone, which she'd set on the wood plank. The porch needed a fresh coat of paint, and she would enjoy doing all those chores and fix it up projects that came with her new job. Sam "Mozart" Reed had always told her she had a restless heart and she should consider settling down and taking a more stable job in the military, instead of volunteering for every dangerous mission she could get her hands on.

Her only fear was that she'd get bored. Of course,

she had the sexy fireman across the street to keep her eyes occupied. He waved as he jogged across the street.

"Hey, I've got some bad news," Brodie said, stopping at the base of the porch.

She tipped her head, staring into those dark eyes that reminded her of the finest warm dark chocolate drizzled over ice cream. "What's that?"

"I've been called in for an overnight shift, so dinner and drinks will have to happen another night."

"It was drinks, and you know where I live." She flicked her hair over her shoulder. It was a blatant sexual move, and she had no idea why she'd done it.

"It will be more than drinks because I cook the best steaks in town."

"And if I'm a vegetarian?" Someone needed to sew her mouth closed, giving her brain a chance to think through the things that she said.

"Then I make a mean veggie platter." He winked.

"For the record, I enjoy a good piece of meat."

His eyes went wide.

"Your mind just went straight to the gutter, didn't it?" She really needed to shut the fuck up. Flirting was one thing, but this banter was the kind of shit that got her into trouble.

"Who? Me? Never. But now that you sent my mind there, I'll remember what you like."

She waggled her finger in his direction. "I think we need to dial this conversation down a notch. I don't even know you."

"I plan on getting to know you," he said with a smile. "I gotta run, but If you need help at all with the move, come knock on my door, just don't ask my roommate, he's helpless."

She laughed. "Are you cockblocking your buddy?"

His mouth dropped open, and his eyes blinked wildly.

"If we're going to be neighbors and occasionally have a drink, you should be forewarned, I say exactly what I think, when I think it."

"I had already figured that out, I just hadn't expected it to be so blunt." He leaned forward, stretching out his arms, resting his hands on the step on either side of her hips.

She cocked her head to the side as he invaded her personal space.

Oddly, she didn't mind.

"And since we're being forthright with each other. Yes. I'm cockblocking my buddy, and unless you flat out tell me to bug off, I'm going to stop by next time I see your car in the driveway with a bottle of wine and a huge steak." He pushed off the steps, turned on his heels, and strolled across the street as if he didn't have a care in the world. He hopped into his pickup truck. Another man, who she assumed was his roommate, equally handsome, slid into the passenger seat.

She fanned herself after the truck took the corner and disappeared onto the main road. Brodie had sent her heart on a tail spin, and that didn't ever happen unless she'd been staring down the wrong end of an AK-47.

"Christ, that is one sexy man," she mumbled. He wasn't quiet six feet, and he wasn't broad, but he was solid, with well-defined muscles. He had that All-American-boy-next-door look, with a dash of badass.

Pushing him out of her thoughts, she sipped her diet soda waiting for the clock to tick to eleven in the morning.

Thirty-two seconds.

Mozart never failed.

And like clockwork, his name appeared on her phone.

"Good morning," she said with a smile, trying to ignore the tightness in her chest. It had been eleven in the morning on this date twenty-five years ago when the police told her and her father that her sister had been found, dead. It had been hard to pinpoint the exact time of death since Amy's body had been so badly decomposed, so Harper used this day as the anniversary of Amy's death.

A year later, her father committed suicide, leaving a young child to be raised by her grandmother.

And now she was gone.

Tears stung her eyes. She'd chosen this day to move into her new house hoping it would ease the ache in her heart. Amy had been seventeen when she'd been murdered, and ten years older than Harper. The gap in their age didn't create a distance in their relationship. However, it felt like Amy had been more of a mother than a sister considering their mother had died from breast cancer when Harper had been fifteen months old.

She didn't remember her mother, but her sister —she could still smell the coconut of her shampoo and feel her loving arms wrapped around Harper like a protective blanket. Even her wonderful grandmother couldn't recreate that sensation.

Her sister would be proud of what Harper had done with her life, and hopefully Amy and their dad were in heaven, if such a place existed, staring down at Harper. Over the years, she'd reconciled with herself that Amy had needed her dad up there more than Harper needed him here with her.

"Are you settled in?" Mozart asked. She'd met Mozart the year he'd brought his own sister's killer to justice.

The same man who took Amy.

Harper had wanted to thank him and never expected the kind of kinship they had developed over the last six years.

"Still waiting for the truck with what little shit I have."

Mozart laughed. "Trust me, you'll start collecting crap quickly."

"How are Summer and April?" Harper had met Mozart's family a couple of times. Truly a blessed man.

"Great. April is talking up a storm. She's turned this man into a pile of mush. Even has me playing Pretty Pretty Princess, not caring that Summer is taking pictures with me sporting blue clip-on earrings."

"I'd pay good money to see that."

"Never gonna happen," Mozart said.

A short silence filled the airway as it always did when they talked of family. They belonged to a club that no one wanted, and the price of admission was too painful to wrap your brain around.

Unless you lived it.

Then it haunted your every breath.

"Don't forget, I know a couple of men on the base. You should look up Ace Enders. He's a Fire Protection Specialist and a good friend of Tex's. He and his wife are good people. Also on his team are Hunter Jackson and Jax Strovos, both married, though I don't know Jax that well."

"You've given me all their contact information, more than once, and after I get settled, I'll reach out."

"I'm sure they will stop by your office when they can if you don't." In the last few years, Mozart had become the only family she had, and she appreciated everything he did for her, but sometimes, she just needed to sink into a quiet space. "What about a Brodie Welch? Do you know him?" Guess right now quiet wasn't on the menu.

"Yeah. I met him at Ace's wedding. He's good buddies with Declan Rivers."

"As in the son of JAG officer Ashton Rivers?" The only reason she knew Corporal Rivers was because she'd been called to testify in a case where he'd been the defendant's attorney. Smart man and scary, too.

The cross of her testimony had been more frightening than the first time someone fired a machine gun in her general vicinity.

"That's the one," Mozart said. "I know Brodie is single, but I think Declan has a girlfriend, or at least he did a year ago."

She rolled her eyes. "Don't you dare try to set me up." She'd never tell Mozart that she had every intention of knocking on Brodie's door, if only to get another look. However, relationships weren't her thing. Not because she didn't like men, or the company of men, but every boyfriend she ever had told her she was emotionally unreachable. The last one would always try to get her to talk more. What the hell was wrong with silence? Why did everyone want to fill it with small talk and stupid shit?

"Having a boyfriend might be a good thing," Mozart said with a slight laugh. "Now that you've gotten that death wish mentality out of your system and took a stable job, maybe it's time."

"You call being an investigator for the Air Force a stable job?"

"Hell, yes," Mozart said.

A moving truck turned down the street. "I've gotta run. Talk soon, okay?"

"Let me know if you want a visitor. I'll be on the next plane."

"Thanks, I appreciate it. Hug April for me."

"Will do."

With that, the phone went dead.

Harper stood, waving to the driver. It was time to start the next chapter in her life.

CHAPTER 3

After a twenty-four-hour shift, the last thing Brodie wanted to do was mow the lawn, especially when the night had been filled with one call after the other, leaving him feeling worse than his hang-over from yesterday.

The only thing Declan ever got weird about was the lawn and landscaping, wanting it to be meticulous, and Declan certainly had a green thumb.

Brodie not so much.

That said, Brodie was a neat freak and couldn't stand it when Declan left out a throw blanket when it should be folded and put away in the cabinet.

So, the idea that the gas can he was absolutely certain he'd put in the back of his truck had somehow vanished, drove him nuts. He'd borrowed some gas from a neighbor, got the lawn and weed whacking done, then crashed for five hours.

Five glorious hours of deep sleep, according to his sleep app, which he'd become addicted to. He'd been surprised by how accurate it seemed to be based on when he did wake in the middle of the night. Regardless, he felt refreshed and after a hot shower and one beer, he had all the courage he needed to meander across the street and knock on Harper's door.

With Declan still sound asleep, Brodie snagged a bottle of red wine, two steaks, and a couple of ears of corn he'd picked up on the way home. This certainly was a bold and forward move, but this chick had taken his breath away, and he wanted to find out more about the woman behind the sexy looks.

She'd backed her SUV under the carport. The forever screen door was the only thing separating him from the inside of her house. Just as he was about to knock, he saw her adorable butt wiggling back toward him through the family room as her arm moved back and forth pushing a mop. In the background, he heard the twangy voice of some male country singer mixed with her sweet voice, though a bit pitchy.

He leaned against the doorjamb and let out a long sigh. “Wanna dance?” he asked.

She jumped, dropping the mop to the ground. “Christ, you scared the shit out of me.”

“Sorry.” He held up the bottle of wine and the steaks. “Are you ready to take a break? We can go back to my place or if you’ve got a grill, I can cook.” He winked. “I’ll do all the clean up too.”

“Does that mean you’ll finish mopping for me?”

“God, no, and I don’t do bathrooms.”

“What good are you then?” She pushed open the door, taking the wine from his hand. “I’ve got a brand-new grill with a fresh propane tank, but you’ve got to hook it up.”

“I’m thinking I might regret coming over here.”

“I made chocolate chip cookies earlier, so I think that might make up for it.”

“Damn sure it will.” He followed her through the family room, where a sofa and a love seat had been staged. A rectangular distressed wood coffee table stood in the middle of the room. Two pictures, one of the beach and one of a turtle, leaned up against the wall.

He tried not to get dirt on her clean floor as he made his way into her kitchen.

Most of the houses in this area were set up the

same way with the kitchen and dining room in the back of the house, three bedrooms of the left side of the family room, and this house was no different, except hers was recently updated with new cabinets, floors, countertops, and other finishing touches that his place didn't have.

The kitchen had been expanded, joining it to the dining room, making it more of an eat-in kitchen. A center island had been added, and the brand-new appliances were all stainless steel.

"This place is great," he said, remembering when the previous owners had begun their remodel. It had been one problem after the next, and it had taken seven months to finish the project. Sadly, the couple that owned the house ended up having to sell when he'd been transferred to the other side of the state.

"It was the first house I looked at. Every house after just didn't hold a candle. I also like the area, like being close to the beach, and work."

"What do you do?" He set the steaks on the counter.

"We can talk about that over dinner." She pointed to the back patio. "Trust me to prep the steaks while you wrestle with the grill?"

"As long as you bring me a glass of wine first."

"Deal," she said with a smile. She set the bottle on the counter and opened a drawer.

Her dark hair had been pulled up into a ponytail. Her jean shorts hung loosely on her hips. An inch of her mid-drift peeked out from between her pants and her crop top. If he had to guess her age, he'd say she was closer to thirty and that was fine with him. He preferred a mature woman but didn't want to go older than himself.

"You're staring." She popped the cork and quickly poured two hefty glasses.

"Just waiting for that." He took the flute she offered and clinked with hers. "Here's to a good piece of meat."

She laughed. "Go. I'll be out shortly."

He took his wine and pulled open the slider. Her backyard was lined with lush, tall palm trees, creating a fair amount of privacy. A small stone patio took up a good portion of the area. Laughing at the fact that the price tag was still on the new outdoor table, he went about his task to hook up the grill and get it fired up so he could burn it hot for a good twenty minutes. Kind of like cleaning new dishes before eating off them.

When he was finished, he sat down in one of the

chairs and sipped his wine, staring at the orange sky as the sun made its descent behind the horizon.

"Here you go," Harper said as she placed a tray on the side of the grill. The steaks were coated lightly with some kind of rub, and she'd wrapped the corn in foil. She also brought out a spray water bottle to help control the flames. Impressive. However, the best part had been that she'd brought out the bottle of wine and topped off his glass.

"Cheers to—"

"If you say meat, I'm kicking your ass out of here," she said with a smile.

"Cheers to good neighbors becoming good friends."

Her lips curled over the rim of the glass as the red liquid flowed into her mouth in an exotic, memorizing dance. One he needed to break quickly.

The steaks sizzled as he slapped them on the grill, keeping the lid open, gauging the temperature, which ran a little hot, so he turned it down a tad.

Harper sat in one of the chairs, angling herself to face him, along with pushing out another chair to prop her feet on. Her long legs with lean muscles tortured his mind with visions of things he shouldn't be thinking about. At least not right now.

His mom and sisters had beat into his brain

never to sleep with a woman on the first date. That wasn't the kind of woman you wanted to spend the rest of your life with.

Why the fuck was he thinking about the rest of his life, plus he knew for a fact his oldest sister had slept with her husband before she even knew his name.

Jesus, Harper had him turned upside down and inside out.

"So, are you going to tell me what you do for a living?" he asked, flipping the steaks and spraying the flame, keeping them from charring the meat.

"I'm an Air Force Investigations Officer."

He snapped his head in her direction. "No shit."

She tipped her glass. "I enlisted when I was twenty, right out of college with a criminal justice degree."

"That's really fucking cool." Being sexy was one kind of turn on, but being smart, and a badass chick, that was something entirely different. "How long have you been an investigator?"

"About a year. I was stationed at Langley for that year."

"What did you do before you became an investigator?" he asked as he put the steaks on the plates she'd provided and joined her at the table. The food smelled like the finest restaurant, only all he cared about was getting to know the lovely lady sitting across from him.

"I started out as a Clerk in the JAG office, but quickly became an MP."

That made him stop chewing for a second. "That is one hell of a tough job."

"Especially as a woman."

"I bet. My twin sister went through hell to become a firefighter. Still does sometimes."

"Is she in the military?"

He shook his head. "She's back in Vermont with the rest of my family."

"Do you have more brothers and sisters?" She cut through her steak, making small bites before digging in.

"Only sisters. My twin, Madison, and then one younger sister, Nora, and my other sister is older."

"That must have sucked being the only boy."

He laughed. "It was interesting, that's for sure, but no. Not really. What about you? Siblings?"

Her eyes glossed over, and her pretty smile quickly tipped into a frown. She raised her hand and cleared her throat. "I had a sister. She died a long time ago."

"Jesus, I'm sorry." He pulled out the chain that

held his dog tags and encircled them in his fingers. No way could he wrap his brain around losing one of his sisters.

"My childhood wasn't a pleasant one," she said with a tremor in her voice.

He wondered if he should change the subject, but that felt rude. He should let her direct the conversation.

She emptied the bottle of wine between their two glasses and leaned back in her chair. "My mother died from breast cancer when I was a baby."

He swallowed. Hard. He wanted to move to the chair next to her and wrap his arms around her, but he suspected that she was the kind of woman, that when she chose to discuss this kind of suffering, needed her space.

"Then my sister was murdered when I was seven."

"Jesus Christ," he mumbled.

"I don't mean to be a downer, but you asked."

He stared into her cocoa orbs, keeping her gaze, trying to convey with a single look that she could talk all night long about whatever she wanted.

And he'd listen.

"I take it that is why you went into this line of work."

She nodded. "It was that or a become a shrink since a year after my sister died, my father committed suicide."

"Fuck."

"That's a good way to put it." She dropped her head back and closed her eyes. "I don't know why I just told you all that. It's not something I share with someone when I first meet them, but today is the anniversary of the day I found out my sister had been killed."

"I honestly can't imagine. I've seen my share of death. Even had a decorated pilot die in my arms after pulling him from a plane crash, but I don't have a clue as to what you have gone through. Can I ask a question?"

She opened her eyes and lowered her chin. "You can ask. I might not answer."

He nodded. "Did they catch whoever murdered your sister?"

"Years later they did. A man who had also lost a sister to the same killer was instrumental in bringing him down."

"Mozart," Brodie whispered, remembering the story well. "I've met him a couple of times. Good man."

"The best."

A long silence filled the night air. The meaty aroma lingered in his nostrils while the crickets sang a sweet song. The sky slowly turned a dark blue as nightfall took over.

"I have a question for you," she said, but didn't wait for him to agree to answer. "What's it like being a twin? Is that connected shit true? Like can you feel what she's feeling or know when something is wrong?"

He held up his hand, showing off three fingers. "I think that is more than one question."

She laughed, waving her hand and shaking her head.

"In answer to your question, yeah, some of the twin stuff is true. I mean, I don't feel her physical pain, but we have a connection that is different from my other sisters. When she was going through firefighter training, she had to deal with a lot of harassment, even today."

"Oh, don't I know it," Harper said with an arched brow. "I'm sure half the people who gave her shit thought they were doing her a favor, toughening her up."

His turn to laugh. "Madison sure as shit didn't need that. If anything, she needs some refinement around the edges, but I suppose that comes from having to fight tooth and nail to be respected in her own profession. One, I might add, she's damn fucking good at."

"You sound like one proud brother."

"I am, and I think you and Madison would really like each other."

"I kind of like her brother."

"Her brother sort of likes you back." His stomach fluttered like a teenager about to see his first boob. He could sit here on this patio, just like this, all night, and be perfectly okay with that, even though his body desired something more.

Hell, he craved something real. Something honest. Something that would lead to something of the forever kind.

"We both must have had too much wine, because we sound like a bunch of saps," she said.

"Well, this sap was promised some cookies."

"You haven't cleaned up yet."

He tossed his hands wide. "Woman, you drive a hard bargain."

"You clean, I'll pour more wine and warm up those cookies."

He groaned as he gathered up the plates, setting them on the tray. "You're making it really hard for me to remain a gentleman."

She waltzed across the patio, her fingers gliding on the side of the table. “I’m about to make it harder.” Her hands landed on his shoulders as he leaned into his body. Her chest pressed against his. “You’re a compelling man.”

“That’s not the compliment I was looking for,” he said, circling his arms around her petite waist. He lowered his head, tilting sideways, his gaze darting from her lust-filled eyes to her plump lips. His mouth brushed hers, slowly at first, tasting the sweetness of her femininity that blended nicely with the wilds of a woman who knew exactly who she was and what she wanted.

She pushed away, taking a step back, her killer smile sucker-punching his ability to breath. For the second time, the damn woman literally took his breath away.

“Don’t forget to scrub the grill,” she said as she slinked from his arms and strolled into the kitchen, glancing once over her shoulder as she kicked her leg up behind her.

“You’re killing me.”

“That’s the point.”

CHAPTER 4

Harper hadn't had this much fun since—hell, since ever.

"You want a job as my cleaning lady?" she asked, sinking into her sofa in the family room. Besides doing all the dishes, Brodie had hung her two pictures and had just finished fixing her coffee table with the wobbly leg.

"You can't afford me." He smiled, still bent over in the center of the room.

She let out a long sigh which sounded more like a moaning dog in heat.

He arched a brow. "Was that from relaxing on the sofa, or something else?"

"Let's just say I like the view." She wished she could say she was loose with the lips because of too much wine, but they'd paced themselves over the last four hours, and she was barely buzzed. Besides, her mouth always acted like a fire hydrant on full blast.

"It's dark outside, there is no view." He eased onto the sofa, his thigh barely touching hers with his hand resting dangerously close to her bare skin.

"I wasn't looking outside." All evening, she'd felt as though she'd known Brodie for months. Years even. They had this comfortable rapport that only came with long friendships between two people who could finish the other's sentence, something she barely had with her best friend.

"Flattery will get you everywhere." He leaned closer, tilting his head. "I like hanging out with you, and I want to do it more often."

"We're neighbors, so I'm sure we'll run into each other."

He traced a finger along her jawline. "That we are." His thumb tugged at her lower lip before he cupped the back of her head, letting his mouth take hers in a slow, intense kiss. He tasted like rich chocolate and a dry red wine that lingered long after you swallowed.

She blinked her eyes closed, pressing her hand on his powerful chest. Her heart hammered, and every cell in her body electrified. Her skin bristled with the need to have his hands—and lips—caressing her most intimate, erogenous zones. She couldn't remember wanting a man in her bed more, and she had a feeling that once she had him, he'd become an obsession. This was not the kind of man you had a one-night stand with.

No.

Brodie was the type of man who seeped into your pores, devouring every molecule until your heart beat as one with his.

He curled his fingers around her hip, shifting their bodies, and she caved to her desires without reservation when she straddled him, cupping his face, diving her tongue deep into his mouth. He certainly didn't seem to mind as he gripped her ass and his tongue intertwined with hers, coating the inside of her mouth with droplets of a promising storm.

She raised the bottom of her shirt, but he stopped her from lifting it over her head.

"As much as I want to see what is under this shirt, people walk around this neighborhood all the time at night and right now, anyone passing by has a perfect view of both of us."

"Not an exhibitionist, huh?" She pushed herself off his lap, holding his hand.

"No, and I hope you're not either."

"Depends on who is looking," she said, pulling him toward her bedroom. While she remained confident on the outside, her insides shook like a scared rabbit hiding in the bushes from a wild fox. She'd always been able to mask her nerves, a quality she'd learned when she was younger and constantly had to prove that girls could do anything. But this was different. It had nothing to do with asserting or establishing her abilities. With Brodie, right here and now, she was taking one of the biggest risks of her life because she believed without a doubt, this man could rip her heart out and leave her bleeding on the side of the road.

"Where are we going?" he asked.

"My bedroom where I have shades."

He let out a deep, throaty groan that tightened her throbbing nipples. "I'm really glad I made an ass out of myself this morning." Grabbing her arm, he twisted her body, heaving it toward his chest. Reaching down, he gripped the back of her thighs, spreading her legs and lifting her off the ground.

"Whoa," she managed before his tongue darted into her mouth. He continued to move effortlessly, kicking open the bedroom door. With her legs still wrapped tightly around his waist, he managed to close both blinds and turn on every light in her bedroom before laying her on the bed on her back, his strong body pressing against hers like a warm blanket.

"I guess you like the lights on."

"I'm a guy. I'm kind of visual that way." He nuzzled his face in her neck as he sucked on her earlobe.

"Then let me give you the optimum view." She rolled him over so once again she was straddling his waist, feeling his hardness in exactly the right spot.

Must have been good for him too since he groaned, gripping her thighs.

She didn't waste any time and ripped off her shirt, unhooking her bra, and releasing her average-size girls, suddenly feeling shy. Never had she worried about what anyone thought of her, or her body. Any lover she'd had, if they didn't like what they saw, or criticized in any way, she easily said goodbye. Anyone who loved her would have to love all of her, or she hadn't the time or inclination to press on.

Resisting the urge to cover up, she let her hands

drop to her sides, her chest heaving up and down with every nervous breath.

Brodie rose up, pressing his hands on the mattress. His hot breath tickled her skin. His dark eyes smoldered as he gently kissed one of her nipples. While his tongue swirled around the hard nub, he never tore his gaze away, leaving her lungs burning, along with her body, as if she were sitting in front of a crackling bonfire.

She moaned as he moved to the other breast. The only thing touching her was his mouth and that was somehow the most erotic thing anyone had ever done.

He cupped the back of her head and drew his lips to hers as he gently rolled her to her back, dotting kisses down her chest. He managed to undo her shorts, rolling the fabric over her hips.

"Shirt for a shirt," she said, wanting to see his naked body in all its glory.

"Sure thing." He yanked his T-shirt over his head then tugged her shorts and panties off in one swoop.

"Whoa, you're fast," she mused.

"Hopefully, not where it matters," he said with a long, slow drawl. He dotted the inside of her thigh with delicate kisses.

Her chest heaved up and down in anticipation of

what was to come. The closer his lips moved up her leg, the hotter her skin became.

He smiled before he buried his tongue inside her, swirling and lapping in controlled strokes.

"Oh my," she whispered. Her body became desperate. She gripped the sheets, tossing her head from side to side, biting down on her lower lip to keep from screaming. She'd had lovers before who brought her pure pleasure, but every single one of them she had to tell them where and how.

Brodie needed no guidance.

"Oh God," she said, raising her hips shamelessly, and he didn't disappoint, finding the spot she needed him to caress the most.

His hands roamed her body like a fine, bold wine hugging the sides of a glass as a connoisseur masterfully swirled the liquid. The fan above her head cut through the air, sending a cool breeze across her perspired skin like the ocean breeze. Brodie's touch was both temperate and tempestuous, leaving her utterly breathless.

Her orgasm built quickly, sending a shock wave from her nipples to her center. If she wasn't mistaken, Brodie smiled against her as she clutched his head, digging her fingers into his scalp, and clasping her legs tight. Her body jerked as her climax continued like aftershocks of an earthquake. The moment she thought she could take a breath, Brodie would add a finger, or do something with his tongue, and it would send her over the edge.

"I need you to stop," she said, pushing his head from between her legs.

"I was just getting started." He pressed feather light kisses on the inside of her thighs, looking up at her with a twinkle of mischief in his russet eyes that had a fiery twinge of orange around the edges.

"Come here," she said, waggling her finger. "Kiss me."

She tasted herself on his lips as she fumbled hopelessly like a teenager with his zipper. She wanted to explore his hard curves and super soft skin in the hope of making his body tense and shudder. She wanted to hear him whisper her name as he stared down at her while she teased him endlessly.

Shit.

There was nothing worse than not being able to disrobe a lover.

Thankfully, without fanfare, he removed the article of clothing. She glided her fingers over the length of him, tracing a path over the tip. All she could think about was guiding him inside her while staring into his eyes.

He pushed from the bed, standing before her with her hands covering him, sliding up and down. His fingers tugged at the strands of her hair that fell over her shoulders.

She loved how he hissed when she rolled her tongue over the tip before taking him into her mouth. He stared at her, his hands tangling in her hair as he let her have her way with him. She'd never wanted to taste a man like she wanted to taste Brodie.

His thigh muscles tensed as she continued to lick and tease him. He moaned louder when her tongue circled the head while her lips were still on the tip. He groaned as she took all of him into her mouth. The desire to please him was stronger than any need she had for herself.

"Now I need you to stop," he said with a throaty voice. He pushed her back onto the bed. "We have a problem since I wasn't expecting this tonight."

"What's that?"

"I don't have a—"

"Condom? I have one around here..." she leaned over the side of the bed and rummaged through her make-up and toiletry bag until she came across a box of three. She laughed as she handed them to him.

"What's so funny?"

"Never mind." Her cheeks flushed.

"No. Tell me."

"Just remembering when I bought those, knowing I had no one to use them with. It's been a while."

"What's a while?" He took one of the foil packages, tossing the box on the nightstand as he climbed onto the bed, lying on his side, hand propping up his head.

"Oh, maybe six months or so."

"I feel your pain." He tore open the condom wrapper with his teeth.

She burst out laughing.

"If you were any other woman, I think I'd be terrified you were laughing at me."

"I am laughing at you," she said, cupping his face. "I've never seen anyone do that before."

"Can't say it was a stellar moment on my part."

"I thought it was studly." She didn't give him a chance to laugh as she pulled the condom from his hand and quickly rolled it down over him as if he were a delicate, malleable piece of wet clay needing to be molded into something beautiful. She pushed him on his back while she slowly, and gloriously, guided him inside. "Oh..." she said with a long, breathy moan.

His hands squeezed her hips so tight, she figured he left his prints behind.

Leisurely, at first, she rolled her hips, rocking back and forth.

He went from gripping her hips to massaging her breasts. His legs tightened underneath her, and she could tell he was doing everything he could to maintain control.

But she wanted him to lose it. She leaned over, her breasts in his face. He took a nipple into his mouth, and she started grinding.

"Jesus," he whispered. He gripped her, holding her, slowing her down, but she continued to grind.

He groaned, his fingers digging into her muscles. "Be careful, I might have to toss you on your back," he said with a soft moan.

"Oh, promises, promises."

The growl that came from his throat vibrated across her body. He flipped her over and rammed himself deep inside.

"Oh my God." She moved against his rhythmic thrusts, digging her fingers into his shoulders. "Oh, yes," she said with a long moan, her hips grinding wildly. An orgasm shot through her, seemingly coming from nowhere.

He groaned as he slammed into her one more time, holding himself steady, his release pouring into her.

Digging her heels into his back, she arched and rode out the pleasure as he collapsed his weight on top of her, kissing her neck, whispering how beautiful and sweet and wonderful she was, and she could listen to him say those things all night long.

She ran her fingers up and down his back as they both tried to catch their breath.

"We have two more, you know," she whispered.

"You might be sorry you reminded me of that."

"Sore, perhaps. Sorry? Doubtful." And with those four words, she knew this would be the beginning of something wild and unexpected.

CHAPTER 5

If Brodie were a teenager, he'd want to go find his best friend and brag about going three times in one night. He rolled to his side and checked the clock.

Six in the morning.

Harper had mentioned she needed to be up by seven for work. That gave him just enough time to run out, get another box of condoms and something for breakfast, since she had almost nothing, so he could wake her up proper.

He slipped from the bed, doing his best not to disturb the sleeping beauty, and found his clothes. Once dressed, he stared at Harper. The sheet covered only one breast, and her leg peeked out from under the covers. Her hair pooled partially over her face.

The space in his pants just got a whole lot smaller.

Carefully, he closed the bedroom door and made his way across the street. He couldn't decide if he wanted to make her one of his famous breakfasts or buy something premade.

His male prowess demanded the latter.

"Making a run for it?"

Brodie jumped at the sound of Declan's voice.

"What the hell are you doing out here? "Brodie tossed his wallet into the front seat of his pickup, giving Declan a dirty look.

Declan raised his mug. "Enjoying a cup of coffee while I watch the sunrise, wondering where the hell my roommate spent the night. Dude, I was worried," he said with a shitty grin and a huge dose of sarcasm.

"Right. Besides I sent you a text telling you I wasn't coming home." Brodie reached in the cab and turned the key. The engine roared to life. He glanced over his shoulder, hoping it hadn't woken Harper. The last thing he needed was for her to think he wanted to avoid the morning after.

No. He wanted a good morning only lovers could share.

"Imagine my surprise to see your truck here all

night, but your bed was never slept in." Declan smirked. "Where, oh where did you sleep?"

"I'm not going to answer that," Brodie said, biting back a smile.

"So, you and the new investigator, eh?"

"Shut up Captain Obvious and you're not Canadian." Being single meant anytime he took a girl out, his fellow firemen could and would harass him. It was always all in good fun. While his ego preferred to be on the other side, his body was quite pleased.

"What's she like?" Declan asked, blowing into his mug. "Besides being smoking hot."

"Did you seriously just ask me that?"

Declan rolled his eyes. "I meant her personality. I can tell by the smile on your stupid-ass face that the evening festivities were mind-blowing."

"Screw you," Brodie muttered as he covered his mouth with his palm, his thumb and forefinger tracing his jaw, as if to erase the evidence from last night.

He liked everything about Harper from her off-color remarks, to her sexy body, but especially the way she held her end of a conversation. Smart didn't cover her intelligence.

"I heard she's in tight with Mozart."

Remembering the look on Harper's face when

she'd talked about her family made Brodie's heart ache. "She knows him well." He put one foot on the runner. "I like her, so don't go doing stupid shit, and if by chance she comes here looking for me, I'll be right back. She's got no food, so I'm getting breakfast."

"Why don't you raid our kitchen? We've got plenty."

"I've got to pick up some other things." He rubbed his jaw, contemplating asking Declan. It wasn't like they've never helped each other out before. "Unless you've got what I need."

Declan raised his hand. "Dude. How many times do I have to tell you, I'm not your type."

"You're not anyone's type and not what I was asking for."

Declan laughed. "I have no condoms and have no need for any, which is about as pathetic as a fisherman with no hooks."

"What about Becca?"

Declan shook his head. "She's smart, a good firefighter, pretty, but I spent two hours listening to her go on about her ex. She's still hung up on him, and I'm not going down that rabbit hole. Besides, she's young and I think needs to live a little."

"Holy shit, Dec, you sound like a Goddamned grown-up."

Declan shrugged. "Better get going before Harper thinks you snuck out on her because that my friend is one of those things a woman will NEVER forget."

Nothing worse than waking up alone after a long night of the kind of sex you only read about in books. Harper pulled the sheet around her body and padded to the window. She frowned when she lifted the shade. Brodie's truck was nowhere to be found.

Maybe he had to work and just didn't want to wake her.

Only when she mentioned what time she had to head in, he said nothing. And he'd just worked an overnight.

Something vibrated on the nightstand. She turned and let out a sigh of relief. He'd left his phone, so he was probably coming back.

Hopefully before she had to leave for work.

She quickly jumped in the shower, letting the hot water roll over her skin, reminding her of Brodie and his tender kisses. Talk about an oxymoron. His lovemaking was both rough and gentle and nothing in between. He'd been demanding, and yet he'd been so giving and kind. She lathered up her loofah and reluctantly cleansed her body and washed her hair.

As soon as she stepped from the shower, she wrapped herself in a towel and checked the window.

Still no Brodie.

She put on her Air Force uniform, something she didn't have to wear, but thought it a good idea the first few times on the base in her new official capacity as an investigator. It also gave her a sense of confidence that right now had taken a hit because she hadn't thought Brodie to be the type to sneak out, even if he'd changed his mind on wanting to see her again.

A thought that stung more than she dared to admit.

Snagging his phone, she made her way into the kitchen when she heard the sound of a diesel engine. Peeking out the picture window, she saw Brodie's truck.

He jumped from the cab and jogged across the street carrying a bag from the local grocery store in one hand and flowers in the other.

She normally wasn't the floral arrangement kind

of gal. She didn't need those types of gestures, but she found this to be sweet and Brodie the icing on the cake.

"Hey," she said, pushing open the front door.

"I was hoping you'd still be in bed," he mused before kissing her cheek. "But this took longer than I thought." He held out the bouquet of flowers. She hadn't a clue about what type, but enjoyed the fresh array of yellow, purple, blue, red, and orange mirage of colors.

"Thanks."

"My pleasure. You do that uniform wonders." He moved past her and into the kitchen. "How long before you have to leave?"

"Half hour," she said, knowing she technically had a little more time than that, but she wanted to get in long before her first meeting.

"Just enough for a quick breakfast, and maybe a quick something else." He emptied the contents of the bag on the counter. A carton of eggs. A box of microwave bacon. Bread and butter. A half-gallon of OJ and the best part, a bag of fresh coffee.

"The quick something else will have to wait, unfortunately." She snagged the coffee pot and filled it with water. "But I will take breakfast. I'm famished."

"Then I guess we'll have to put these to good use later." He set a box—a large box—of condoms on the counter.

"You're feeling fairly confident that there could be a repeat of last night."

He glanced up over the bowl as he cracked an egg. It splattered out on the countertop.

"Relax, cowboy, I'm just messing with you." She patted his biceps.

He yanked her into his arms. "I owe you a proper good morning kiss."

"That would have been in bed, while we were still naked."

He arched a brow. "But then you wouldn't have had a good breakfast before heading off to fight crime."

"Next time, I'll go hungry."

He growled before taking her mouth in a soft, but commanding kiss that didn't last nearly long enough as the pan sizzled on the stove, waiting for its eggs.

"Finish making the coffee," he said, letting his lips linger on the side of her face. "Someone kept me up half the night."

She laughed. "I think it was the other way around, but whatever." She filled the pot with water and measured out the coffee while stealing glances at Mr. Sexy with his ruffled bed hair and the same clothes he had on last night. He whisked the eggs with the precision of a surgeon. She couldn't think of one thing she didn't like about Brodie, and that scared the crap out of her.

"What are your plans for tonight?" he asked as he dropped the bacon into her microwave.

"More unpacking and obviously grocery shopping."

"I can help with the unpacking and if you want to text me a list, I have to go to the store anyway today."

She folded her arms across her chest and leaned against the counter. Her grandmother told her that if a man seemed too eager, or too good up front, then she should run for the hills. Every man had a flaw, and if they didn't show it quickly and up front, they were most likely hiding one of the darker traits of the male species.

Of course, her grandmother had been married to a gambler and a cheat and she'd never remarried, nor had a long-lasting relationship with another man again.

"What's wrong?" Brodie asked as he dumped the

eggs on two paper plates and pulled open the pouch containing the crisp bacon.

"Huh?"

"You're crinkling your forehead." He waved his hand over his forehead. "My sisters all do that when they are deep in thought or troubled by something." He pushed the plate across the counter.

"I haven't even known you for twenty-four hours and you're offering to go grocery shopping for me?" She turned, not wanting to focus on the confused expression on his face. She poured the coffee into two mugs and sucked in a large breath before facing him. "Why don't we start off with a walk later this evening."

"I understand," he said, smiling.

Why the hell was he grinning?

"Do you?"

He nodded. "I'm in no hurry for anything. I like being with you, and I certainly don't want that to end, so if it means slowing things down to a steady walk, I'm good with that." He held up a piece of bacon. "But I still have to do my own shopping today, so really, I'm just being neighborly."

Before she had a chance to respond, his phone blasted some heavy metal song she didn't recognize.

"Shit," he mumbled as he raced across the room to where she'd left his phone on the counter by the door.

"That is a horrible noise."

"The only one that would wake me in an emergency," he said as he tapped his phone. "Boss, what's wrong?"

She picked at her food staring at Brodie's back.

"I'm on my way."

"What's the matter?" she asked.

"There's a fire. A bad one. I'm sorry, I've got to run." His face contorted as if someone had punched him in the gut.

"Why do I get the feeling its more than a bad fire?"

"The house belongs to a fellow Air Force Protection Specialist. I'll call you later." He turned and gripped the door.

"Brodie?"

"Yeah?" He glanced over his shoulder.

"Be safe out there and please, text me or call me and let me know you're okay, and what's going on."

"Will do."

With a that, Brodie raced across the street, his buddy, Declan, meeting him in the driveway. In a matter of a minute, the truck peeled out of the driveway.

"Well, shit. I'm going to spend my day checking my phone, worrying about man I barely know, yet know in ways I'm sure no other woman does."

CHAPTER 6

"Jesus Christ," Brodie muttered as he rolled his truck to a stop two blocks from Jonathon Battle's house on Cricket Boulevard only ten miles south of St. Patrick Air Force Base. Fire trucks from both the base and a local station lined the streets along with a few police cars and an ambulance.

Flames still burned tall from the partially caved-in roof. A cloud of black smoke billowed toward the sky like a thick coat of coal. A partially charred Jeep with melted red paint and flat tires was parked under the carport along with a brand-new Harley that looked more like a pile of twisted metal than a motorcycle.

"That's not good," Declan said with his Air Force badge in his hand. "Do you see Jonathon?"

Brodie looped his badge over his neck and shook his head. "Ace and Jax are over there." He pointed at the back of the ladder truck. While his team hadn't been on call, this was one of their own.

Brothers to the end.

Ace waved them over while other firemen raced to contain the fire. Hoses were held in place as water spewed over the blaze. Two of his buddies from the other crew ran past with axes in their hands, the intensity etched into their eyes more noticeably pronounced.

"Do we know what happened and where Jonathon is?" Brodie asked, scanning the area, his heart hammering in his chest.

"No idea on both accounts." Ace must have been at the base when the call came in because he wore the standard Air Force Fire Protection Specialist T-shirt.

"Fuck." Brodie didn't like Jonathon, and he made no bones about it, but watching his house go up in flames, well that sucked.

God, he hoped Jonathon was perhaps in the back of the ambulance, being checked out with nothing more than a few bruises. Or maybe talking with an officer down the street. "Who called it in?"

"His neighbor," Jax said, standing with his hands

on his hips, shaking his head. "He signed off the base at midnight, having done a half-shift for someone else. He told Henderson he was headed home because he was doing another half-shift this morning."

"He didn't show up for work," Ace said, pointing toward the carport. "No one has seen him."

"You think he's inside?" Brodie sucked in a deep breath, letting it out slowly. A fire that burned that hot with that kind of smoke, could kill a grown man in his sleep before the flames got to him.

Brodie shivered at the unpleasant thought.

"Hey, boss," Becca yelled as she jogged from the front yard. "Garret says they can't get to the bedroom, and Jonathon's not answering his phone. It goes straight to voicemail."

"Shit," Ace said as he raked a hand through his dark hair.

"The fire is under control, but it will be hours before we can get an investigative team in there." Becca pulled her hair into a tighter ponytail before swirling it into a bun on top of her head. "I asked one of the officers if they could come over here and report back to us what they found out from the neighbors. Shouldn't be too much longer."

"Thanks," Ace said with a nod.

A few shouts from the front of the house caught Brodie's attention. The sound of wood snapping cut through the hum of the hoses. The firefighters took a few steps back as two ran from the front door.

The ground shook, sending sparks into the sky like fireflies that had been set free.

"Maybe Jonathon crashed at some chick's house. He's always got a girl on his arm," Declan said with little to no conviction in his voice.

Brodie watched helplessly as the black smoke turned grey and dissipated into the morning sky. It appeared the flames had been put out, but they still would continue to douse the fallen structure until it no longer produced dangerous amounts of heat.

"Hey, boss," Jax said, pointing to the barricade the police had made at the corner. "Who is that?"

Brodie looked over his shoulder. "Harper?"

"You know our new Investigator Officer?" Ace asked with an arched brow.

"She's my neighbor. We met when she moved in." Brodie continued to eye Harper as she flashed her badge to one of the local officers, who puffed out his chest. A few of the locals didn't like working with the military and he was sure, some took issue with women in positions of high authority. Glancing around, he figured she outranked every man from the Air Force here.

"She's tight with a buddy of mine I know through Tex," Ace said.

"Yeah. Mozart. I met him at your wedding." Brodie nodded at Harper when he caught her gaze. "Did you call her in?" He glanced at his watch. It had been less than an hour since he'd left her house. That was barely enough time for her to get to the base and then drive to this neighborhood.

"Nope," Ace said, planting his hands on his hips. "But it's certainly not unheard of to have someone from her office at the scene when it's one of our own."

"But you're thinking the same thing I am." Brodie's stomach churned as he tasted the scorched wood and metal with every hard swallow.

"That fire burned too hot and fast for me not to be suspicious," Ace said.

"The call came in with a description of smoke coming from the windows," Becca said. "When Max's team arrived, fifteen minutes from the time of the call, the fire was out of control and had taken the entire house."

Brodie's heart skipped a beat as Harper stepped closer. "Hey, Brodie. Declan," she said, then turned her attention to Ace. "I recognize you from pictures Mozart has shown me over the years."

"It's good to finally meet, but the circumstance sucks." Ace held out his hand. "Have you been introduced to Jax or Becca?"

Harper shook her head, greeting them with slight smile.

"They're going in, boss," Becca said, taking a step toward the house.

"Jax and Declan, go with her. Stay out of the way but keep your eyes and ears open. I want to know what they find."

"Yes, boss," Declan and Jax said in unison.

"So, what have you been told?" Ace might be the quiet, reserved type, but he never held back any punches. Always direct and to the point. Which was why he was being made Captain of the entire fire department on base.

"Not much other than Jonathon Battle is missing, and the fire is suspicious." The uniform fit Harper, her demeanor commanding and professional. "If we find a body, or we suspect the fire was started intentionally, I'm here to formally take over the investigation from the locals."

"That's being a bit proactive without knowing what happened," Ace said.

"There's more to it, isn't there?" Brodie asked.

She nodded. "But I can't divulge that information just yet."

"Fuck," Ace muttered. "My arson team can't do their job unless we know exactly what we are dealing with."

"We don't know that we need your arson team. But if it comes to that, you will be the first person who will be given clearance."

"Clearance? Jesus, Harper, what the hell is going on?" Brodie held her stare and not once did she blink. Nor did her tight facial expression change. "You're investigating something else, aren't you?"

"Brodie, I can't discuss an ongoing investigation with you, or anyone right now," she said with a slightly softer tone.

"Can you at least tell us if Jonathon is the center of the—"

"No. I can't." She held his stare and gave nothing away. A trait expected of a seasoned investigator. But considering he'd just slept with her, he'd hoped he'd be able to find her tell, or she'd give him some kind of sign. "If, and when, it's deemed appropriate for you to know anything, I'll inform you."

Jesus. Right now, he resented the professional side of Harper as much as he respected it.

"Boss!" Becca called. "We got a body."

Brodie's heart plummeted from his chest to the center of his gut. His pulse slowed for a half a second before it raced wildly out of control.

"Ace, who is on your arson team?" Harper asked.

"I've got three trained specialists besides me. Brodie here is one. Jax and Hunter are the other two."

"Is Hunter here?" Harper asked, letting out a long breath.

"No," Ace said.

"Get him here, pronto. I'll call my boss to make sure I can grant all of you clearance. Be prepared to go in as soon as the house cools enough and please, for fuck's sake, start getting the locals out of here. This is officially an Air Force crime scene."

Brodie slipped on his boots and set his fireman's hat on his head. It had been forty minutes since the first responders had found a body, which had yet to be identified as Jonathon's. The Air Force Medical Examiner had yet to remove the body since they had to make sure the house was safe for everyone to enter, which Max's team had done about five minutes ago.

Brodie, his fellow arson team members, and Harper had gathered at the back end of the ladder truck. The crowd that had gathered had been reduced in numbers, but the local news stations had set up camp at the corner, trying desperately to get the military police to talk, but that was never going to happen.

A few local fireman and police officers gave statements about how the 'incident' had been turned over to the Air Force authorities since the casualty had been a military man, but they were even more in the dark than Brodie.

"Are you going to fill us in on the scope of the investigation?" Brodie asked what Ace, Hunter, and Jax were all thinking.

She shook her head. "We'll do a full briefing back at the base where I know it will be secure. Too many civilians wandering around with big ears."

"I don't like the sound of this," Ace said as he pulled his fireman coat around his body. "How do we know what we're supposed to be looking for if—"

"I want you and your team to focus solely on the fire. Where and how it started. What caused it to burn so hot and fast." Harper took the jacket Brodie offered, along with the hard hat.

"You've got to give us something." It wouldn't be the first time Brodie went into an investigation knowing very little, but not when murder might be on the menu.

"I agree," Hunter said. He'd arrived at the scene fifteen minutes ago and other than Ace, he had the most training when it came to arson.

"All I'm going to tell you right now is that a week ago, my office opened an investigation into Jonathon," Harper said.

"About what?" Brodie didn't want to let it go. He couldn't. They needed to know if they should be looking for something specific.

"Look." Harper let out a long breath. "Today is my first day, and I'm not completely up to speed. But more importantly, we don't know how far what we are investigating goes, so you're just going to have to wait until we're on base. Ace, you're with me."

"Yes, ma'am."

"Dude told me Harper was one tough cookie," Hunter said, slapping Brodie on the back. "I hear she's your neighbor."

"Yep." Brodie followed Ace and Harper across the front yard. Just ahead of them was the medical examiner with one member of his team and a gurney. They all paused for a moment, the reality of the situation sinking in. "What the hell do you think Jonathon was into?"

No sooner did the words leave Brodie's mouth, then Harper glanced over her shoulder, shooting him a dangerous look.

He nodded, acknowledging he needed to keep his trap shut and that made him even more nervous. He scanned the area, making a mental note of all the military personnel, wondering if someone had either set the house on fire.

Or was in cahoots with whatever crap Jonathon had gotten himself into, which honestly didn't surprise Brodie. Jonathon had known issues with authority his entire career, and his reputation preceded him wherever he went.

"If looks could kill, I'd say you'd be flat on your back," Jax said.

"I hate that look. Claire gives it to me every time I let the kids fall asleep in our bed." Hunter had two rug-rats and was probably considered one of the cool dads. Of course, he was independently wealthy, so that helped since he had a big house, with a pool, and every toy a kid could ever desire.

"Scarlet gives it to me when I let Rusty play video games too long," Jax said.

"No. She does that because you're the one playing too long," Brodie said as he stepped across the threshold.

"Whose side are you on, anyway?" Jax said as more of a statement than a question.

"Ace and I will take the bedroom side of the house, you three have everything else," she said right before she took the turn down the hallway, Ace two paces behind.

In silence, Brodie, Jax, and Hunter examined the family room, or what was left. Half of the roof lay on top of what Brodie assumed to be a coffee table, sofa, and an electric recliner. He knelt next to it, inspecting the wires that had burned into the socket on the floor, but there was nothing indicating it could have started with that.

"Look at that." Jax pointed to the gaping hole that used to be the outside wall in the back of the house. "Does it look like it burned inward to you?"

"Yeah," Brodie said, stepping over the rubble that was still warm.

"But it burned up and out over here," Jax said, standing where the kitchen would have been. Instead, all that was left was a shell of a fridge and an oven. The counter had slipped right off the cabinets, which were scorched. Everything had a black layer of wet soot.

"It looks like the fire started on the other side of the house," Hunter said. "What direction is the wind blowing?"

"East to west," Jax said.

"Make sense since there is less damage over here." Brodie stood by the door that went to the side porch. He took his glove and tapped at the wall. "Pretty solid. Not very warm at all. I bet this wood isn't singed all the way through."

"That means point of origin has to be in one of the bedrooms," Hunter said as he headed in that direction, while taking pictures of the destruction.

"Two years ago, Jonathon failed his drug test," Brodie said, shaking his head.

"I remember that." Hunter stopped in front of what used to be the bathroom door and snapped a few images. "He'd been on leave for twenty-one days and owned up to smoking a little weed. He got a slap on the wrist."

The sound of feet crunching over debris caught Brodie's attention. He glanced up to see the medical examiner pushing a gurney with a sheet over what couldn't be much of a body, considering the size of the mound.

Out of respect, they stood at attention, saluting as what the assumed was Jonathon's body was removed from the house.

"At ease," Ace said, standing in the doorway.

Brodie swallowed hard, remembering his last encounter with Jonathon, which ended in a confrontation and a fist fight, not to mention some pretty nasty verbiage they both had exchanged. He didn't like the man, but Brodie didn't wish Jonathon any harm. No one deserved to die in a house fire.

"I'm going with the medical examiner," Harper announced as she appeared from the bedroom, her face pale even though perspiration beaded across her forehead.

"Harper?" Brodie started, staring into her dark, horror-filled eyes.

"Finish here and then meet me at the base. It's going to be a long day," she said.

Brodie wanted to race over and hold her. He had no idea how many dead, burned bodies she'd seen, and it didn't matter.

Every single one would haunt you for the rest of your life.

Ace nodded toward the hallway before following Harper out of the house.

Brodie carefully stepped over more wreckage as he made his way into the main bedroom. "Jesus," he muttered.

There was nothing left of the room but black, charred material. The roof had completely caved in, and what should have been a door to the back patio was another cavernous hole. The temperature of the room had to be five degrees hotter than the rest.

He peeked his head out and scanned the patio.

"Holy fuck," he said.

"What is it?" Hunter raced to his side.

"That gas can right there."

"Yeah, what about it?" Hunter asked.

"It's mine."

CHAPTER 7

“Where’s Brodie?” Harper dropped a thick file on the conference table.

At the far end of the room, Ace leaned against the wall with his arms folded across his chest.

“Interview room two,” Ace said with a tight jaw. Mozart had told her, or maybe warned her, that Ace was worse than a mother bear when it came to his crew.

“And Declan?” she asked. Changing the name from interrogation to interview didn’t change that she was about to question her new neighbor, and her lover.

Well, one night didn’t make for anything but a one-night stand.

"Room one." Ace's short answer went along with her frazzled nerves.

"Are you alright with Edwin leading the questions?" Normally, she wouldn't pass off any part of her investigation to another officer, but in this instance, it was probably best to protect the integrity of the case.

"I'm okay with it, but I don't understand why you're not doing it. You barely know either one of my men."

She sucked in a deep breath. If she didn't tell Ace about her little slumber party last night, she could make things worse in the long run.

"I want to watch from the viewing room." She'd learned early on that sometimes you could learn more about a suspect and their potential role in a case by observation instead of taking the lead role.

"I want to be there too."

"Not a problem, but I think I need to tell you something."

"What's that?" Ace cocked his head. Mozart had also told her that Ace could read people better than most, and based on his narrowed stare with one slightly curved eyebrow, he might have already suspected.

"Brodie and I, we... how do I put this?"

"I get it." Ace raised his hand. "Is that the real reason you don't want to question my men?"

"That's one reason."

"Can you be impartial?" he asked.

"Can you?"

"Absolutely not," he said with conviction. "I've served with those men for a decade. They have saved my life more than once. They are my brothers. I also know the angst between Brodie and Jonathon. It goes back a few years."

"What is the source of their problems?"

"Jonathon," Ace said matter-of-factly.

"There has to be more than that."

Ace nodded. "Nobody likes Jonathon. He's a cocky son-of-bitch who doesn't follow the rules, and he's put us in danger with that attitude."

She pushed the folder across the table. "This is all the information I have on Jonathon and our investigation into him."

"Give me the abridged version."

"Five years ago, his half-brother robbed a bank in North Carolina."

Ace pressed his knuckles on the table and leaned forward. "I didn't know he had a half-brother."

"His name is Archer Henderson. Archer was the product of an affair their father had. He was apprehended shortly after the heist, but the authorities could never get him to give up his accomplices or where he hid the money. Three months ago, Archer's new high-priced attorney managed to get a retrial based on some questionable police work, and the conviction was overturned."

"So, Archer is a free man and you think that Jonathon was one of his partners in this bank heist."

"Jonathon was on leave during the time of the robbery, so it's possible, but he had an alibi and even though his military career isn't without scars, he was dropped as a potential suspect."

"But that's changed?"

"When his brother was released, the FBI kept a close watch on Archer, and he made several phone calls to his brother and a week ago, stopped by for a visit."

"Seriously?"

"That's when the Feds lost him and contacted us. My office questioned Jonathon about his brother, and he told us that there is no love lost between them and when he showed up, he kicked him to the curb. However, since Archer has become a ghost, and the FBI found some inconsistencies with Jonathon's story, we started combing through his bank records, but nothing out of the ordinary popped up until recently."

"And what's that?"

She flipped opened the folder. "On the day his brother was released from jail, he bought a Harley, with cash, and it's not the one parked under the carport. Where is that bike?"

"I don't know of any such purchase," Ace said, pushing off the table. "But I'm not close to the man. I honestly do my best to avoid him."

"One other strange thing we noticed was that Jonathon started withdrawing larger amounts of money than he normally had in the past, and this also started after his brother had been released."

"How much money?"

"A thousand here, two grand there. All checks made out to himself or cash," she said.

"So, what are you thinking?"

"The Feds believe he's helping his brother and when I spoke the agent in charge, he's positive his brother must have killed him for the money."

"Which means perhaps he was part of the heist or had been holding the money all these years," Ace said as he paced at the end of the room.

"Or didn't know he had the money. Jonathon bought that house six months before the robbery."

"That's a lot of what ifs with nothing substantial to back it up."

She nodded. "And then there is the issue of the gas can, which Jax and Hunter's report clearly states an accelerant had been used."

"But the can was stolen out of the back of Brodie's truck."

"So he says." Her heartbeat became irregular as the words fell off her tongue.

"And you don't believe him?" Ace asked.

Of course she believed him, but she had to follow all leads. "Brodie has had more than one run-in with Jonathon and the most recent resulted in a fist fight. I have to consider that whatever ties Jonathon might or might not have with his brother, has nothing to do with his alleged murder."

"Come on. You're a smart lady. You really believe that?"

She shook her head. "But I can't ignore the gas can, now can I?"

"No. I guess you can't," Ace said, running a hand through his hair. "Alright, let's get this over with so you can rule out my men."

"Hey, Ace," Harper said as she gathered up the file. "Can I count on Brodie to tell the truth, even if he thinks it will damage my reputation or my working on this case?"

"I'd lie for my wife, so be prepared for anything."

Brodie had expected Harper to be sitting across the table in the interview room, not some guy from her office named Edwin.

"How well do you know Jonathon Battle?"

"We're not friends, but we're both Fire Protection Specialists."

"Are you enemies?"

Brodie had seen Edwin around the base. He was kind of hard to miss at six foot seven, but he hadn't had any interaction with him until today.

"No." Brodie decided it was best to keep his answers short and to the point.

"But you got into a fist fight the other day, correct?"

"We did," Brodie admitted, trying to contain his frustration. He figured he would be sitting in this chair for another hour, answering the same questions over and over again.

"Why?"

"He crashed a party he wasn't invited to and

made a dickhead comment about one of my co-workers."

"What do you mean a dickhead comment?" Edwin asked, his hands clasped together on the metal table.

"A sexist remark about a new crew member on my team. I didn't take too kindly to it, not to mention I was drunk." Brodie had always been more sensitive to those types of things because of his twin sister. Didn't matter if whoever said the derogatory comment didn't mean it.

"So, you just hauled off and punched him?"

"Not exactly. I asked him to leave, politely, but he got in my face, that's when I hit him."

"What happened next?" Edwin asked in the same monotone voice he had used for the last question.

"We both tossed a few more before my buddies broke it up and then Jonathon left."

"When did you next encounter Jonathon?"

"I didn't. That was the last time I saw him," Brodie wouldn't feel bad about the fight, but his heart did drop to his stomach knowing that Jonathon was dead.

"So, he didn't ask to borrow your gas can?"

"Nope." And here came the fun questions. The

ones where Edwin would try to get him to admit to something, or not.

"How do you suppose it ended up at his house?"

"I don't know," Brodie said, and that was the truth. He'd run through that day five times in his mind while waiting to be questioned, and he hadn't a clue.

"When did you last see the can?"

"I put it in the back of my pickup, but I got called in to cover a shift, so instead of getting gas, I drove to work."

"With the gas can in the back of your truck?" Edwin asked as he leaned back in his chair.

"Yes."

"When did you notice that it was missing?"

"When I stopped to get gas after the overnight shift. I had to borrow gas from a neighbor to mow the lawn," Brodie said, shifting in the hard, cold seat.

"Your neighbor will corroborate your story?"

"Yes."

"What did you do last night?"

Fuck. If he lied, he'd look guilty as hell when it came out. If he told the truth, he would be putting Harper in a difficult position. "I had dinner with a neighbor."

"What neighbor?"

"Does it matter?" Brodie grappled with his conscious. The gentleman in him wouldn't kiss and tell. Things with Harper were too new, and he wanted more time to see where things might go. Telling Edwin about his evening would put her under the microscope and right now, he figured that was the last thing she needed. "The fire wasn't set the night before."

"Alright then, where were you this morning?"

"Home." Hopefully Brodie wouldn't have to elaborate. Lying by omission seemed less like lying.

"All morning?"

"No. I went to the grocery store before I got called to the fire."

"How long where you gone?" Edwin asked.

"Forty-five minutes."

"And what store did you go to? I mean, where was it in relation to your house and Jonathon's."

Well, that was a humdinger. "Two blocks from Jonathon's."

"That would be enough time to start a fire, especially by a man who knows more about fires than the laymen."

"That's all true, but I didn't start the fire. I've got the receipt at home for the groceries, with timestamps. My roommate saw me leave for the store, and return. May I go now?"

"I'm going to need to get the receipt."

"Not a problem," Brodie said behind gritted teeth. Five o'clock couldn't come fast enough.

CHAPTER 8

"I'm glad you're here," Harper said as she sat down on her porch steps next to Brodie. The sun hit the horizon with a glow of orange and pink streaks reaching like fingers across the sky. The crickets had begun their evening song, and an owl hooted in the background.

"I thought we should talk." He twisted open a beer and handed it to her.

She gladly took a long swig. The cold bubbles hit her throat in a refreshing waterfall of flavor. "You could have told Edwin that I was the neighbor you were spending time with."

"First, it's not his business, so for as long as I don't need you for some sort of alibi, he can go fuck himself."

"I'm his superior, so you're telling that to me too," she said with twinge of sarcasm.

"Not you, but your office." He twirled his thumb over her knee. "Second, I like to keep my private life just that and honestly, we don't even know what this is."

"Thank you, but next time, don't lie, especially not if you're trying to protect my honor. I'm a big girl."

"I didn't lie."

She took his hand in hers, intertwining their fingers. "You omitted the truth, which isn't much different. What would you have done if he pushed?"

"I have no idea," Brodie admitted. His bourbon eyes captured her gaze. Behind the intensity of his stare lingered a fusion of anger and sadness. Underneath that, she could see his kind soul. Brodie was the type of man that people flocked to. He was cool under pressure and offered comfort in times of need.

Silence filled the night air. A few minutes ticked by as they sipped their beers and held hands. They had already slid into a level of comfort that came from years of knowing the other person and how they responded to life-changing events.

Yet, there was an awkwardness that still had yet

to be addressed. The kind of unease that came with keeping something from the one you loved.

Only she didn't love him.

Heavy like, she'd admit to.

"You know I can't talk about the case with you," she said.

"Which is why I'm not asking anything. I wouldn't do that to you. I care about you too much."

"Yeah, and we're back to that," she whispered. Leave it to him to address the one elephant that sat between them.

"So, you think this is all going too fast?"

"I don't know what I think," she said, staring at a little girl riding her bike down the street in front of her parents. Her little legs pumped, and she waved enthusiastically. "But I do know one thing."

"What's that?"

"I don't want to sleep alone tonight, and I suspect you don't either. You lost one of your own today."

He nodded, rubbing his free hand across his face, his index finger and thumb meeting in the middle of his chin. "Jax called and said Jonathon's body was burned so badly, they still have to make a positive ID."

"We'll know for sure by morning, if not sooner.

When I left, the medical examiner had just gotten the rest of Jonathon's records." She thought it strange that Jonathon used mostly doctors outside of the military, except for the required physicals.

"You're talking about the case," he said.

"Nothing that you couldn't find out on the base by asking around, so not really." It would be difficult to hold back, considering she wanted to bounce things off Brodie. His deduction skills were sharp, and he'd be an asset to the team from an arson standpoint. But mostly, she just wanted to be able to curl up in his arms and let the intense emotions she coiled behind her heart a chance to rear their heads so she could stay focused.

"Staying with you tonight would compromise the case."

"As of this moment in time? No, it won't."

"I'm a person of interest. I probably shouldn't even be here right now."

She swallowed. Both Brodie and Declan had been named in the case, but neither one was a suspect. However, as a seasoned investigator, she knew how quickly cases like this could take the most unexpected twist. "You didn't kill Jonathon." She had to believe that. Trust that this investigation would prove that the killer had simply snagged the gas can from the back of Brodie's truck.

"No, I didn't," Brodie said. His words lingered like a thick cloud ready to dump large rain pellets to the ground.

"I'm sorry we had to put you through that today."

"You're just doing your job." He rubbed his thumb across her lower lip. "I wish I could get my hands dirty on this case. I didn't like Jonathon, and I've never apologized for that, but no one deserves to die like that. I was in that house. Even though I was pulled out quickly, I know that fire started right there in that bed where Jonathon had been found."

Harper wanted to stop Brodie, but a liquid glaze coated his eyes. He needed to talk, and she could listen.

"I can't help but think someone doused him, and the house, with gasoline and lit a match. That would explain a lot," he said, his voice thick with grief.

"I'm going to find out what happened, and I'm going to nail the bastard," she said.

A slight smile lifted the corners of his mouth. "That I believe without a shadow of a doubt."

"Come on, let's go inside." She stood, tugging at his arms.

"Are you sure? Because I won't say no, but I came over because I thought we needed to clear one thing up. Since we've done that, I still don't want to put you in a bad spot."

"You're not. Come on. I'll order a pizza."

He nodded, then followed her into the house. Once inside, he leaned against the doorjamb, letting out a long, audible sigh.

"What is it?"

"I just can't believe he's gone. I mean, holy fuck, I think I'm going to miss the asshole, and it really sucks that the last encounter I had with him had been a fist fight." He covered his eyes with his forearm as the back of his head hit the wood.

She hadn't known him long but she knew him well enough that rushing to his side to comfort him would be the last thing he wanted. She understood that.

"Jonathon had made a nasty sexual comment about Becca. I was glad he hadn't said it front of Declan. He would have gone off and whaled on him long before I did."

"Are Declan and Becca an item?"

"No. Declan was hurt real bad, and I guess so was she. He's being gun-shy and a moron, if you ask me, but maybe they both need a little time to heal." He lowered his arm. "What do you like on your pizza?"

"Meat," she said with a smile, knowing the mood needed to be lighter. Brodie had said what he needed to. He would work through his emotions one step at a time. She admired his ability to stay level-headed through all of this when someone half the man he was would have gone off half-cocked.

"There is a great place a few blocks from here, but they don't deliver."

"Are you talking about Michael's Little Shop on the corner of third?" she asked.

"That's the one." He took the few bottles of beer left in the six-pack and placed them in her fridge. "It's a nice night for a walk."

"It sure is."

They ordered a large pizza, joking that what they didn't finish tonight, they'd have for breakfast. Harper picked at the crust on her third slice, sitting on the back patio of Michael's. It was bigger than she had thought, and the outdoor seating area faced the west, showing off changing colors of the sunset.

During dinner, it had gone from pink to a reddish purple before turning the night sky blue-black, speckled with bright stars.

Throughout dinner, the conversation remained light, mostly discussing the songs that played in the background and favorite concerts they had attended over the years. A few military men and women and came went, all stopping to stay hello to Brodie, and ask him what had happened to Jonathon. Thank God, Brodie told everyone he didn't know much, making sure everyone left her alone.

"Wow. This has to be the best pizza I've ever had and that includes my grandmother's. She's rolling over in her grave as we speak." Growing up, Harper practically lived on pizza. Her grandmother worked two jobs, one of which was making her special pizza sauce for a local restaurant. Harper's first job at sixteen had been in that same establishment, working side by side with the woman who raised her.

Brodie tossed his napkin to his paper plate. "People drive from over an hour away, just to grab a slice."

"I'm not surprised. The atmosphere, for essentially a fast food place, is great too."

"I could think of better places to take you on a date," he said as he leaned back in his chair. "There is this place called The Canal House across the bridge. I've never been there, but I'm told the steaks are out of this world, and it's right on the water."

"Is it fancy?" Not that Harper didn't enjoy dressing up occasionally, but she much preferred a pair of jeans with a stylish shirt.

Brodie shook his head. "Not from what I've been told. They also have some kind of band playing every night. We should definitely check it out."

"I'd like that."

Her pulse kicked up when the corners of Brodie's mouth curved into a seductive smile. She couldn't think of one thing she didn't like about this man, which also made her a tad nervous. Every man, even the good ones, had a flaw.

"We'll save for when this case is over."

He had to go and remind her of all the paperwork sitting on her desk. All the interviews that had already been conducted that she needed to review and potentially assign new interviews.

The patio door swung open and caught her attention. "Shit," she muttered, eyeing Edwin walking through the door. His timing couldn't be any worse, or any more on cue based on the direction of the conversation.

"What's the matter?" Brodie asked.

"Don't look now, but Edwin just walked in."

Brodie didn't take heed as he glanced over his shoulder. "Who's the chick on his arm?"

"No idea."

Edwin pulled back a chair for the blond woman in four-inch heels, tight shorts, a sleeveless tank top, and a cowboy hat. If her over-the-top make-up, including blue eye shadow, didn't draw all eyes in her direction, then that hat certainly would.

"She's...interesting," Brodie said.

"Yes. Everyone can see her ass cheeks falling out of those shorts."

Brodie turned his head, lowering his chin. "I wasn't looking at her ass."

"I was," Harper said with a smile and a short laugh as she leaned across the table. "She doesn't seem to be his type." She'd met Edwin a dozen times before her transfer to Patrick Air Force Base and each time, Edwin came off a little left of kilter. In their first meeting, he tried too hard to impress her, which made him appear insecure. The second meeting, he came across arrogant when discussing one of his current cases, which happened to have been a minor incident where Jonathon had disregarded protocol. At the time, Edwin had not been brought in the loop about the other investigation.

Edwin's personality seemed to waffle between socially awkward to socially annoying, but thus far, his investigative skills, and professionalism, were admirable.

"Opposites attract?"

"Ya think? I mean, he's nerdy and she's...she's..."

"Not?" Brodie questioned with a daring smile and slight twinkle in his mocha eyes.

"Shit," she whispered. "Here he comes." She shoved one last bite of crust into her mouth, wishing it were a shot of Fireball.

"Hello, Major Dawson. I see you found the hot spot in town," Edwin said, towering over them like a skyscraper with his hands on his hips. "Captain."

"I think off base you can call me Brodie."

Harper stifled a laugh. She had forgotten that technically, Brodie outranked Edwin. Though, kudos to Edwin for doing the respectful thing.

"All right, Brodie it is," Edwin said. "Harper, can I have a word with you?"

"Sure." Harper stood and followed Edwin to the far east side of the patio. No wonder his date wore fuck-me heels. His damned head reached the stars. “What’s up?”

“I put this on your desk, but since you’re out with him tonight, I think I should tell you what we uncovered.”

“If this was urgent, you should have paged me,” she said, not hiding her annoyance.

“I don’t have all the information yet, but we found a sealed record on Brodie. I’ve gone through the proper channels to find out the nature of the record.”

“Did the military purge the record, or locals?” she asked as she swallowed the lump that had formed in her throat. She shouldn’t be concerned about this at all. It wasn’t uncommon for minor juvenile offenses to be buried upon entering the military.

“We don’t know yet.”

“How is that possible?” During an investigation of a capital crime, her office should be able to gain any information about a person of interest without a large number of hoops to jump through.

“It appears it was actually supposed to be expunged, so whatever the offense, it could be off the books by now,” Edwin said.

“No expunged record is ever untraceable,” she muttered. She once had a case where the suspect’s criminal behavior as a child had been erased from all databases.

Except the military's.

Of course, it had been the military who concealed the information, which in turn bit them in the ass since he had turned out to be a serial rapist.

She glanced over her shoulder. Whatever Brodie had done as a teenager, it had to be something stupid, like streaking. Or maybe drunken behavior at the prom. Something that almost every idiot teenager had done, only he had been the unlucky bastard that got caught.

"The only thing we have been able to find is a case number. Everything else has up and disappeared."

"How did you find that if there isn't a paper trail?" she asked.

Edwin pursed his lips, and she knew she wasn't going to like his answer. He'd done that once before today, when he'd gone and done something without her approval. Not that he needed her to sign off on everything, but as lead, and his superior, she needed to know everything. In a case like this, she couldn't afford to be blindsided.

"I got a tip to check into his background."

"What!?" She cocked her head, glaring at Edwin. "When?"

"Right after you left the office," Edwin said with a scowl as he scratched the side of his neck. "We got a phone call from someone who wouldn't leave their name, so I checked it out, thinking it would lead to nothing, only it led to something and now I'm waiting."

"Goddamn it, you should have called me the second that call came in. Was it a male or female?"

"Woman. We couldn't get a trace."

"What number did she call?"

"That's the odd part. She called my private office."

"That means she didn't go through the switchboard and has access to direct lines. Not many civilians know those numbers," she said softly as her mind turned over a million possibilities. "You said the information is on my desk?"

He nodded, holding up his phone. "Legal is supposed to call me as soon as they find anything."

"You make sure you call me before you take your next breath, got it?"

"Yes, ma'am," he said.

"Is there anything else?"

"No, ma'am."

"All right. I'll see you in the morning, if not before." She turned on her heels, sucking in a deep breath and putting on her best smile. She'd wait until they were in her living room before she let the questioning begin, and she prayed that Brodie would have answers that didn't make matters worse.

CHAPTER 9

One didn't have to be a Sherlock Holmes to deduce that someone had put a nasty bug in Harper's ear.

That someone had to have been Edwin.

Ever since Brodie and Harper had left Michael's, she'd been distant. Cold, actually. On the walk home, she'd kept her arms folded and when he looped his arm around her waist, she tensed. He remained silent until they reached the steps to her front porch.

"Want to tell me what is bothering you?" He didn't see the point in beating around the bush.

"I need to ask you a couple questions, but since I don't have all the information, I'm not sure where to start."

"Let me guess. Your lacky there found out about

my arrest record." Even if that wasn't the case, he figured it could become a sticky situation, and he might as well get it out there, even though everyone that mattered already knew.

Everyone but Harper.

And she mattered more than he cared to let on.

"He found a sealed record."

"Come on." He took her by the hand. "This conversation is going to require a glass of wine and a couple of chocolate chip cookies."

"This isn't a light-hearted conversation. Edwin is pushing you to be more than—"

He pressed his finger over her pink, plump lips. "Let me tell the story and if you want, I'll call the legal department myself and see if they can get the documentation."

"Edwin is under the impression it was supposed to be expunged."

"It had been." Brodie hadn't thought he'd ever have to tell this story again and technically, when he entered the Air Force as well as Fire Protection Training, he was not obligated to inform the military of his crime. However, his father recommended he come clean with the senator who made the recommendation for him to attend the Air Force Academy. Telling the truth made all the difference in the world then; he hoped it did the same in the eyes of Harper. "However, before the paper trail had been completely destroyed, I opted to inform the military."

"Smart move, since they would have found something anyway."

He nodded as he uncorked a bottle of wine and poured two generous glasses. Harper eased into the sofa, tucking her feet under her butt.

"What was funny was that at first, they couldn't find the records, so they were concerned I was covering up something worse," he said, kicking his feet up on the coffee table, letting his leg roll to the side, so his skin would touch hers.

"So, are you going to tell me what happened, or continue to beat around the bush?"

He chuckled, but quickly cleared his throat. "I've always had a fascination with fire." He held her stare, wanting to be able to read her reaction. Some people might not appreciate how he ended up doing what he did.

"Isn't that true of most firefighters?" Her lips puckered over the thin rim of the wine glass. The liquid flowed into her mouth like a river of sweet raspberry chocolate.

"That and being an adrenaline junky, but my

obsession caused a couple of 'incidents.'" He used the term his mother had every time she told the story, which wasn't often.

"Couple?" Harper asked with an arched brow.

"Like all boys, I played with matches. When I was ten, I was lighting them in the bathroom and dumping them in the waste basket and left without thinking to put water on them first."

"That's really stupid," she said.

"I know that now, but I was a small child. Anyway, my parents had to redo the bathroom that year, which made my sisters royally pissed off because it took six months. But I got to meet some pretty cool firemen and from then on, I had only one goal in mind."

"You said your twin is a firefighter. Does she have the same preoccupation with fire?"

"Oh yeah, the second major fire, she and I were in cahoots."

"I really don't like the sound of that." Harper took a thick gulp.

"The first fire we set was a total accident, but we damn near blew up the science wing during my freshman year of high school." He laughed, even though it wasn't really funny, but reminiscing about some stupid shit back in the day often required a good chortle. "Basically, my twin and I were messing with the gas burners and melting different things, only we hadn't paid attention to some of the chemicals, and let's just say we're more than lucky no one was injured except for my sister and me. We suffered some minor burns."

"And that didn't teach you to stop playing with fire?"

He set his feet on the floor, twisting his body to face her head on. "I'm not proud of what I did next." He'd been mortified the second the police slapped the handcuffs on his wrists, and the shame and guilt that squeezed his heart when his twin had been shoved into the back of the police car still curdled his stomach. "A few months later, right around my fifteenth birthday, my sister and I decided to light our old treehouse on fire so we could put it out."

"At fifteen?" Harper asked. The two words were laced with discontent.

"We really believed we knew enough about firefighting that we could control it, like an experiment, only it didn't happen that way, and we burned down half the forever wild area behind our house."

"Holy shit." She pounded her chest with her fist as she coughed. "That's a fucking big deal."

"Handcuffs big deal," he admitted, rubbing his

wrists, remember the feel of cold metal digging into his skin. "My sister and I were given probation and five hundred hours of community service. We also had to go through a psych evaluation and mandatory counseling."

"I'm assuming they decided you're not a sociopath with a liking for arson."

He'd laugh at her comment, only her sarcasm came off as though it were masking a truth. As if she believed he was the same boy who did a stupid thing.

"My sister and I learned a lot about ourselves during counseling and honestly, if we need to make lemonade out of this, it gave us both a passion for using our obsession for good. I love putting out fires, not starting them, except for during training."

"I'm amazed the D.A. was willing to help you have your record sealed."

"It wouldn't have happened if my sister and I hadn't thrived during our probation and community service. They had us working in the fire department and with EMTs. Mostly we cleaned up after them, but we developed a love and respect for the profession. If being totally honest, knowing what I know today, I think I'd still set that fire. I'm the man sitting here on your sofa because I got to see what life could be like if I continued to make stupid mistakes."

She set her glass on the table, glancing toward the ceiling, as if it had the answers he had yet to provide.

Although, he had no idea what those questions might be.

"What are you thinking?" He took a risk and laced his fingers through hers, setting their hands on his thigh.

"I need to know if we're going to find anything else besides what you just told me."

"As far as my record goes, that's it."

She snapped her gaze to his. "There's more?"

"If you call being suspended from school for fighting, then that's the more. I wasn't a perfect adolescent. I had my fair share of black eyes and trips to the principal's office." He let out an exasperated breath. He could understand her judging him for setting a fire. Hell, he judged himself. But he'd paid his debt, and he served his country with pride and a clean record since then.

"I'm sorry, I don't mean to sound like a jerk, but this could potentially move you from the person of interest right to the top of the suspect list."

"Do you honestly believe I could use a fire to kill

someone in cold blood?" He yanked his hand away and abruptly stood, snagging his wine glass before it toppled to the floor.

"Did I say that? Or even imply that's what I thought?" She glared at him. Her opaque orbs, partially covered with her eyelids, radiated the kind of hurt that fueled anger.

"No. I guess you didn't." He turned and stared out the window. His truck was parked across the street, right behind Declan's sport SUV. The kitchen light glimmered, and Declan sat at the table with what looked like Becca, but Brodie couldn't be sure from this distance.

Harper's tender fingers curled around his biceps. Her sweet lips brushed the back of his neck. "I can't treat you any differently than I would if I wasn't sleeping with you."

He took her hands and wrapped them around his middle. "I hope you don't hug other people on any kind of list like this."

She laughed. Finally, the tension had been cut. Not broke, but it was better than ten minutes ago. "You mentioned you might be able to get all the pertinent information for me about your arrest?"

"I can," he said, twisting his body so his chest

was against hers and his lips so close, he could taste her vanilla lip gloss.

"Any chance you could make that call now? I want to get a jump on it before Edwin goes and says shit he shouldn't."

"Sure." Before he made that phone call, he wanted to make sure she still felt the same and the only way to do that, was to kiss her.

A soft moan vibrated from her mouth to his as his tongue parted her sweet lips. Her fingers dug into his back, giving his muscles a taste of what was to come.

He took her by the shoulders, stepped back, and pulled his cell from his back pocket. "Hey, Siri, call General Van Trotten, mobile."

He tried not to smile at the wide eyes staring back, but it proved impossible. Not everyone had a General's personal cell phone, much less the Director of the Department of Fire Protection.

He tapped the speaker so she could hear everything. He didn't want there to be any doubt in her mind what kind of man she was sharing a bed with.

"Well, if it isn't Brodie Welch. How the hell are you, son?"

"I'm doing okay, sir," he said, swallowing the thick lump.

"I'd say you're up a creek with a broken paddle," the General said. "I'm sitting here staring at paperwork requested from some assistant to the new Investigative Officer on your base."

"I know," he admitted.

"Can you tell me why an assistant is demanding I give him your sealed information and requesting it go directly to him, and not his supervisor?"

"What the hell?" Harper muttered, then quickly covered her mouth.

"General, meet the supervisor, Major Harper Dawson."

"It's a pleasure. I take it you don't know of the request?" the General's voice bellowed over the speaker.

"I was just informed, sir. My assistant said the information was on my desk, but I didn't know he went directly to you."

"Well, now you know," the General said. "What would you like me to do?"

Brodie trusted his brothers, his fellow firemen like he trusted no others. But the General had his back from day one and helped make it possible for him to attend the Air Force Academy in the first place.

"Can I have a digital copy sent directly to my

email?" she asked.

"Sure can. It will come with top-clearance protocol, password and encryption protection. A letter will be attached outlining under what circumstances you are allowed to divulge this information. You will have it in a couple of hours. We can't have one of our best men's reputation destroyed. That said, I've seen the evidence in the case thus far, and I understand, as I'm sure Brodie does, that you have a job to do, and you'll do it to the best of your ability. And I'm confident that you will find the real culprit."

"Thank you, sir," Harper said.

"Anything else?"

"No, sir," Brodie said. "I appreciate the time."

"Anything for you, son. You saved my life. I owe you."

The phone went dead.

"Holy shit. You're the snot-nosed kid that pulled him from a burning ski lodge when he and his family were on vacation."

Everyone knew the story, but no one knew who the seventeen-year-old boy had been that risked his own life to save that of a decorated General. Brodie never wanted to take credit, or get a medal, all he wanted to do was continue to save lives.

The General helped him do that.

CHAPTER 10

"You're really one of the good guys, aren't you?" Harper posed the sentiment as a question, but she meant it as statement of fact. Everyone had those few not so stellar moments in life. Lord knew she had her fair share of mistakes. She had no right to judge, and Brodie had paid his debt.

More importantly, he made it right by paying it forward.

"I'm not a bad one," he said with a wink. His hands massaged her lower back as they swayed to a romantic country song that whispered through the speaker in her bedroom.

His lips brushed the side of her neck, just under her ear. She shivered.

"Are you cold?" he asked.

"Just the opposite," she mused.

"Shall we take off all your clothes, then?"

"You don't have to ask me twice." She raised her shirt over her head, tossing it to the floor.

With swift hands, he unclasped her bra, letting it fall to her feet.

"One might think you've had some practice with that piece of fabric." She couldn't remember a time in her life where she felt a sense of contentment since her sister's murder. Not even when Mozart had given her the closure the doctors told her she needed.

There was no closure when one horrific act changed the course of her life. The emptiness she felt from her sister's murder and her father's suicide left a burning hole in her heart, body, and soul. Nothing could ever fill it. Nothing made her feel like a whole person.

Brodie changed that. Not that he took all the loneliness away, but right now, in his arms, he helped ease the pain that haunted her entire existence.

"Not really," he said as he traced a line with his forefinger from her chin to the center of her nonexistence cleavage, his smoldering gaze keeping her hostage. "Most of my life they scared the shit out of me. I mean, my bathroom was filled with bras, and panties, and other girly things. I swear, I went to school smelling like cucumber or coconut."

"I bet it smelled all sorts of manly on you," she whispered, pressing her lips against his neck, enjoying the vibration of his throaty moan. Sliding her hands under his shirt, she splayed her fingers across his tight stomach. It twitched and tensed under the slight pressure. The contrast of his soft skin and hard muscles sent her body reeling.

"If you say so." He cupped her chin with his thumb and forefinger. "You're a special woman, Harper Dawson."

She opened her mouth to protest, but his kiss rendered her speechless. His tongue swirled around hers, spreading a blanket of warmth across her body like a hot shower. Her nipples puckered under his gentle touch. The room spun around them as if they were the center of the universe. Digging her fingers into his shoulder blades, she deepened the kiss, turning it to desperation, as if she'd been starved, and he were the only thing that could satisfy her hunger.

He cupped her face, and the second their lips parted, a flicker of doubt kicked into her mind.

She blinked open her eyes. "I want you to know I'm not the kind of girl that jumps into—"

He shut her up with a short kiss that ended way too soon. "I know the kind of woman you are, and I like everything about you."

The corners of her lips curled into a half-smile. Her heart swelled as if it were pumping life into the darkness of her childhood. "Anyone ever tell you you're the sweetest man ever?"

"You might not think that in a few minutes, because I'm done teasing you."

She gasped and before she could catch her breath, he had her stepping out of her pants. Dropping her head back, she closed her eyes as he kissed the tops of her feet, licked her ankles, and molded her thigh muscles with his strong hands. His hot lips heated her skin. Every cell in her body exploded like a mini volcano.

He glided his fingers up the curves of her legs, gently grazing her swollen nub, making their way over her stomach. He pinched her nipples while his teeth nibbled on her earlobe.

She'd never been shy in the bedroom, or shy about her body, but she often didn't boldly reach into a man's pants, grabbing the length of him and holding on as if it were her lifeline.

She sat on the edge of the bed, fumbling with his pants, her mouth eagerly waiting to taste him.

"Jesus," he muttered, his fingers tangled gently in her hair.

She tasted and teased and shamelessly took what she wanted. Brodie was like no man she'd ever met before. His sculptured body was finer than any work of art, but it was the man behind the body that took Harper on a sharp turn that she'd never experienced before.

Every other road she'd been on with a man was a dead end, leading them nowhere, with nothing to look forward to except a goodbye.

The path with Brodie was lined with endless possibilities, and if she were to ever fall in love, it would be with someone like him.

"Harper," he whispered, lifting her into his arms. "You're making me crazy."

"I love doing that."

He let out a deep growl as he took one of the condoms. "This is the part where you might not think me so sweet anymore."

"Oh, really?" God, she loved his playfulness.

A wicked smile appeared on his face. "Turn around and bend over the bed, please."

Christ, the man said please. Could anything be sweeter?

With anyone else, she might have been slightly embarrassed as she did what he asked. Fisting the sheets, she braced herself, only she hadn't expected to feel his soft tongue between her legs.

"Oh my God," she said with a long moan. He kissed her body intimately, holding her stomach in one hand, caressing her ass with the other.

She'd never wanted a man more and wasn't above begging.

"Brodie, please," she said, her voice an octave higher than normal.

"Your wish is my desire," he whispered, bending over her and pressing his hardness against her, entering slowly, inch by inch.

Everything in the room blurred as he tortured her with unhurried strokes as if they were out for a leisurely walk.

She glanced over her shoulder. "I thought you were done teasing me?"

"You don't like this?" he said with a wicked grin, moving his hips slightly.

In response, she rolled her hips.

His eyes rolled as his fingers dug into her hips.

She did it again.

This time he groaned as he glided his hand down her belly, his fingers barely grazing her hot nub. His thrusts, while still controlled, came at a faster pace, as did his breathing.

Clenching herself around him, she tried to hold onto her climax, savoring the build-up as he became anything but measured.

His finger rolled over her in an endless circle of pleasure.

"Harper," he whispered in her ear.

She bit down on her lip as her climax spilled out. A wave of intense heat tinged her body from her head to her toes.

It went on and on like the ocean crashing into the beach. Every time she thought she might be able to catch her breath, another surge took her body.

It wasn't until Brodie released his own climax with a guttural groan and collapsed on top of her did she have any reprieve. Even then, with every breath Brodie took, or even the slightest of movements, her body reacted with an aftershock.

"A man could get used to this," he said, rolling to the side, taking her into his arms and kissing her. It was a tender kiss, filled with the promise of love.

Love.

She let out a long sigh.

She needed to dial this back a notch. Anything that moved this fast couldn't end well, and God, she needed this to last forever.

The first night Brodie spent the night, he'd snuck out for breakfast, which he knew Harper appreciated, but he'd be damned if he didn't get to watch her wake up.

He tucked his hands under his cheek and stared at her. Her sable hair pooled around her head. Carefully, trying not to disturb her, he brushed it back so he could see her gorgeous face.

She sighed as her eyelids fluttered open.

"Good morning, beautiful," he said.

"What time is it?"

"Not quite six."

"I've got to be to the base by seven thirty." She rolled to her back, reaching her arms over her head while she stretched.

"I do too. I've got a twenty-four-shift coming up." He kissed the tip of her nose. "Otherwise, I'd say let's ride in together."

Her eyes went wide. "Like we need to give people something to talk about."

"No one is talking. At least not my buddies."

"Maybe not, but word travels fast and with the case..." her words trailed off as she slapped her forehead with her hand. "Shit, I didn't check my email before going to bed. I wanted to be able to ream my assistant out and enjoy telling him to get off your ass."

"You talking like that is just turning me on." He pulled her to his chest, letting her know just how much.

"Oh no, you don't." She wrapped the sheet around her body and shimmied from the bed, leaving him exposed. "Oh my," she said. "No. No. No." She shook her head. "I will not let you distract me again. I need to get in the shower."

He pulled the comforter over his body. "I can join you in the shower and wash your back."

"I know where that will lead and as much as I'd love it, I really need to get to the office early, preferably before Edwin."

"I'll go put on a pot of coffee and start some eggs."

"You are the best."

"I aim to please." He winked, then groaned as she dropped the sheet and padded to the bathroom. If she had been any other woman, he might feel rejected, but he understood she had a job to do and needed to get at it. Besides, five times in two days, that might as well be a world record. He laughed at himself. He couldn't care less how often. The best part about being with her, was just being with her. He had no idea how to explain it other than, simply being in her presence made the world a better place.

He found his clothes and made his way to the kitchen. Once the coffee machine started percolating, he checked his phone.

Two texts from Declan and a voicemail from Ace.

He responded to Declan first, letting him know that yes, they would be going to work together, no, he didn't need breakfast, and yes, he knew his record was being called into question.

Which was the voicemail from Ace.

He texted him, letting him know he could call because Brodie would never call this early. Too many little kids that might be sleeping, and his wife was pregnant again. It wasn't easy being a military wife and even harder when shifts were often more than a day long.

His phone rang immediately.

"Hi, Ace," he said as he whisked the eggs. "How's the family?"

"Alex mouthed off to the teacher at school, so I

had to ground him. He's not very happy with me right now. Charlie has an ear infection, so he kept us all up half the night. And if my bride doesn't get her wish to have a girl, I think she's going to chop my head off, but otherwise, damn wonderful, thank you for asking."

"Alex is seven. What the hell did he say to the teacher?" Bodie sprayed the frying pan with some Pam before tossing the eggs in.

"He got into it with a boy in school who is picking on someone else. The teacher was trying to explain to him that while she appreciates him standing up for other children, he needed to get an adult before taking matters into his own hands."

"He's going to be one hell of a young man with his boy scout attitude."

"Not boy scout, more like vigilante, but yeah, it will serve him well when he's like twenty-five."

"The apple doesn't fall far from the tree."

"No, it doesn't," Ace said. "But I didn't call to shoot the shit about my family."

"I told Harper everything, and the General sent her the official paperwork."

"I'm sorry this is being tossed in your face again."

"It's really not a big deal, except for that damn stupid gas can. Harper can't tell me a damn thing, and I sure as shit haven't asked. I wouldn't do that to her."

"There isn't anything to tell. The only problem is, they have no one else to look at besides his brother, and he's MIA, but I've called in a few favors, and Tex found some interesting news. He's going to send it to Harper."

"What's the news?"

"He found a paper trail to an offshore money account in Jonathon's name."

"How much money?"

"The more important question is: why was it closed the day after his death?"

"That is odd, now isn't it," Brodie said as he slid the eggs onto two plates. "I take it Tex is sending all this to Harper directly. And not her office. I think her assistant has it in for me."

"Tex said he'd bypass channels and make sure Harper gets it before anyone else."

"Thanks."

"Brodie!" Harper's voice screeched.

"I'm in the kitchen," he said. "Look man, I gotta run. I'll see you on base shortly." He tapped the off button and set the phone on the table.

Harper stood in the hallway, wearing only a pair of dress slacks and her bra. Her wet hair dangled over her shoulders, her face white and her mouth hanging open.

"What's wrong?" He raced to her side, curling his thick fingers around her shoulders. "Harper, are you okay?"

She shook her head. "Edwin just called. He's questioning an eyewitness right now."

"And?"

"That witness is saying they saw your truck and you at Jonathon's right before the fire started."

CHAPTER 11

"Who the fuck do you think you are?" Harper didn't bother to close the conference room door before laying into Edwin. "Not only are you jeopardizing this case, but I have half a mind to take you right off it and suspend you for insubordination." Actually, that is exactly what she intended on doing, only she wanted to see how Edwin would respond to the threat.

"Hey, I'm not the one screwing our best suspect," Edwin said loud enough for the entire office to hear. She suspected that included Brodie, who sat in the hallway with a guard. At least it wasn't in handcuffs.

She ignored the jab and still left the door open. Dealing with Edwin and his mishandling of the case needed to be done in public, even if it meant a few whispers about her love life behind her back. She had the upper hand, only she was the only one who knew it. Well, her, Mozart, and Tex. They had been the ones to suggest outing Edwin. At first, she didn't want to do it, but then Mozart took the 'trust me' tone, and that meant he suspected more than the intel he handed her but didn't have the proof yet. "The second someone came forward as a potential witness, you should have informed me. Instead, you went behind my back and made a judgment call that should have been made by me, the Officer in Charge."

"We needed to vet her story," Edwin said. "Time is of the essence in a case like this. I did what you would have done, had you been doing your-"

"I wouldn't finish that statement if I were you. You took it upon yourself to question the witness and deem her story credible without doing a full check." She tossed a file on the table.

"That's not true. I followed standard—"

"Did you ask me to sign off on an official statement regarding Captain Welch?" She folded her arms and tapped her foot, waiting for an answer.

Edwin stared at her with pursed lips. "You weren't here, and when you are out of the office I'm in—"

"Only when I'm on vacation are you in charge. You made this decision last night. You interviewed a potential witness without my knowledge. Not even a phone call or text. Standard procedure would have been to contact me with all aspects, and this wasn't a situation where you needed to act so fast you took me, your superior, right out of the loop. We've got one of our own dead. Murdered. And you're accusing a decorated officer. That is not something this office takes lightly."

Edwin went to close the door, but she put her foot in the way. Tex had found out that Edwin had been up for this job, but he'd been passed over, for the second time, partly because he often went rogue, doing things his own way, and twice he'd mishandled a case, though each time, he got nothing but a reprimand.

This time, things would be different. Being a go-getter was one thing, but she needed team players, not cowboys who wanted to make headlines.

"We have an eyewitness that puts Captain Welch at the scene—"

"Your witness saw nothing because she wasn't even there." She flipped open the folder, exposing a picture of a woman named Ronda Young driving her car through a parking lot across town.

"What is this?"

Harper tapped the photograph. "That's your witness fifty minutes away at the time she said she saw Captain Welch."

"That's impossible." Edwin shoved the papers away. "You can't even tell that's her, and she did tell me she let her daughter borrow her car this week."

"That's funny, because her daughter hasn't shown up for work since the fire, which is odd since she was sleeping with our dead fireman." Thank God for Mozart and his buddy, Tex. She needed a man with Tex's skills in her office.

Edwin opened his mouth then snapped it shut.

"You didn't know that piece of information, did you?" She picked up the image and shoved it in front of Edwin's face. "That's your witness. Clear as day. And the time stamp. Her story doesn't fly."

Edwin held the picture in his hands, his lips drawn in a tight line.

She wasn't going to wait for him to try to fumble his way out of this one. "You had me bring Captain Welch in after you officially named him as a suspect before doing due diligence with the witness. You're lucky I got wind of it before the statement left this office. I've scheduled a hearing for next week regarding this matter, so until then, consider yourself on leave. You are not to come near this case, or any other one for that matter. Now, I could have you escorted out, but I'm not going to do that to you."

Edwin stood tall, his jaw tight. "You're making a mistake. There is history between Jonathon and Brodie. A dangerous one. Not to mention Brodie is a conv—"

"That's enough." She stepped closer, raising up on tiptoe, and kept her voice so low only he could hear. "I know what is behind those sealed records, you don't. So, say something like that again, and I will bring you up on so many charges, it will make your head spin. Now get the fuck out before I have an MP slap handcuffs on you."

Edwin visibly swallowed, then turned on his heels. She waved to one of the MPs she'd brought in to make sure Edwin left. A full investigation was officially underway into his practices as an Air Force Investigative Officer.

She took in a few deep breaths as Ace and Brodie made their way down the short hallway.

"Wow," Brodie said as he stopped two paces away. "I wish you could have told me all that on the way in."

"I didn't know all of it until I got to my desk," she admitted. She'd been overwhelmed with information the second she entered the office. Between what Tex had found and the reports on Brodie's adolescent adventures and what the General had forwarded, her head spun like a toy top.

She pinched the bridge of her nose, hoping to hold back the headache threatening to render her utterly useless.

"There is a lot to process, and I need some time to go through everything," she said. "In the meantime, Brodie, I need you to stay on base."

"His shift is covered," Ace said with a nod. "Besides, he and I have some paperwork to cover before he takes over as Crew Chief."

"Thanks," she gave Brodie a weak smile, knowing that everyone in the office had been stealing a glance here, a stare there, all wondering if they were indeed sleeping together.

Well, it was none of their damned business, but she needed to keep things professional while in her office. Letting Edwin go off was a means to an end, though she wasn't quite sure what that end was just yet.

"I'll be on base until tomorrow morning," Brodie said.

"Thanks for coming in, and I'll be in touch." She

wanted to reach out and touch him, but that would just add fuel to the office gossip chain.

Thankfully, Brodie didn't need any extra prodding and understood her concerns.

She watched him waltz down the hallway in his Fire Protection Specialist boots, pants, and mock T-Shirt, filling them out like a perfect wetsuit after it's been molded to your body in the water.

"Louis, follow me," she said to the newbie investigator. Talk about green. This was his first assignment after going through training and instead of starting as an MP, he'd worked as a clerk in the legal department.

"Yes, ma'am." Louis was barely twenty-five, but he seemed eager to learn the ropes. She'd only been working in the office for a couple of days, but she'd seen the way Edwin treated those below him, and she for one planned on changing how things worked in the office.

"How familiar are you with this case?" she asked as she stepped into her office. The stacks of files next to her computer didn't help the pounding between her ears.

"Honestly, other than what you told me this morning, I don't know jack shit, ma'am."

One thing she valued more than anything on the

job was honesty. "Are you afraid of hard work and long hours?"

"No, ma'am," he said with such enthusiasm it made her heart flutter a little faster.

She rifled through the papers covering her desk until she found the information she was looking for. "Here is access to all of the files on Edwin's computer. I want you to go through his work email, his—"

"Ma'am?" he stared at her with wide eyes.

"There shouldn't be anything personal on his work computer. If there is, ignore it, but I'll need you to notify me, okay?" If Edwin had used his military computer for anything personal, she'd have more to toss at him, and at the very least, she wanted him removed permanently from her team.

"Yes, ma'am."

She really wanted to tell Louis to cut the ma'am crap, but she knew he wouldn't. Not on his first week under her tutelage and certainly not on his first case. She needed fresh eyes and a keen sense. Not someone who worried about what to call her.

"Focus on everything Edwin gathered on the murder of Jonathon. I want you to prepare a report for me in a couple of hours, and then we can discuss and create a plan moving forward."

“I can do that.” He stood, taking the stack of papers she offered.

“I’ll get security to bring you his laptop and files.”

“Thank you,” Louis said as he stepped from the office. “I won’t let you down.”

“I look forward to hearing your thoughts. Please shut the door.”

Once in the privacy of her small office, she let out an audible sigh, but it was interrupted by the phone.

“This is Major Dawson,” she said.

“Dawson, this is Derek in the ME’s office. We’ve got something for you that changes everything.” Derek rushed the words so that they blended together in an almost incoherent pattern. “You’re not going to believe this, but the body found in the fire isn’t Senior Firefighter Johnathon Battle.”

“What?” She rubbed the inside of her ear. “Who is it then?”

“His brother, Archer.”

CHAPTER 12

When Ace shouted the words: *you're back on,* Brodie wanted to break out into the moonwalk, a dance move he didn't too often admit to being able to do. But instead, he ran outside and did a back flip. It seemed manlier.

But it was then tainted by the realization that Jonathon Battle and his girlfriend, Ronda Young, were missing, and a man had been murdered.

Brodie ran a hand through his hair before putting on his fireman's hat. He followed his buddies Jax and Hunter into what was left of Jonathon's home. They knew the fire had been set in the bedroom. They knew gasoline had been used on the body and bed, which is why it had been difficult to ID the body. The only other thing they knew was that Archer had been arrested and convicted of bank robbery before it was overturned on a technicality.

And the money was still missing.

Brodie stepped into what used to be the kitchen. A smile tugged on his lips when he saw Harper. "Hey," he said.

She nodded, handing something to a young man he'd seen in the office, though he hadn't a clue to who he was. "How does it feel to be back?"

"Mixed emotions," he said, planting his hands on his hips and scanning the room. As an arson specialist, their job had been to assess the fire.

They'd done that. But Harper decided having them around to help in her investigation might give her stronger leads. He wasn't so sure about that, but he was happy to do his part. "Anything you want us to look for besides the murder weapon?" The autopsy report showed that Archer had been shot in the head at point-blank range. The bones in his shoulder showed a possible stab wound, and in his hand was a possible entrance and exit wound that could have been caused by another gunshot.

"That would be the needle in a haystack," she said, fingering her long ponytail.

"So, basically, we're just waiting for something to prick our asses."

"What?" she asked, scrunching her nose.

"My mother would say that all the time when my dad would use that quote. Of course, we always had to remind her that hay was prickly, so it didn't make sense."

Harper laughed. The sweet sound cut through the rubble and eased the lingering knot in his stomach.

"I do have something interesting to show you that Louis found."

"Who is Louis?"

She pointed to the kid she'd been talking to a minute ago, who was now following Hunter around like an eager, little pup. "He started in my department three months ago. He's been treated like shit by Edwin the entire time."

"What about the person you took over for?"

"He left two months before I could leave my last post. Edwin was in charge, and he thought he'd be handed the job." She tapped her finger on the tablet in her hands.

"That's a shitshow to walk into."

She nodded, holding out the tablet. "The last person we can find that saw Jonathon or his girlfriend was the same grocery clerk that saw you."

"When?"

"The morning after you beat the shit out of Jonathon."

"I did no such thing." He rubbed his jaw, remembering Jonathon's nasty right hook. "I got two punches in, at best."

She shook her head. "Here's the interesting part." She used her thumb and forefinger to enlarge the image on the screen. "Look here."

Holding the tablet, his hands trembled. "That's Declan's gas can."

"And that's Ronda filling it at the grocery store gas pump, the day after your party."

"Shit," he said, rubbing his jaw. "You think they killed Archer?"

"It's the strongest theory, but here's the kicker."

Brodie almost didn't want to know. He had yet to wrap his brain around the idea that Jonathon might still be alive.

"The day of your party, Ronda emptied her bank accounts to the tune of ten grand."

"That's a lot of money, and I can't think of a logical reason to do that unless she had a big purchase or something," Brodie said. The most money he'd ever taken out was five grand to pay cash for his first truck when he'd been eighteen years old.

"In today's world of PayPal and Venmo, what would be the point in carrying around that much cash? Most places these days don't even want to deal with it, preferring credit."

"This is a crazy thought, but has anyone looked at the court transcripts from Archer's trial and subsequent acquittal?"

"I've got one of my clerks combing through the documents," Harper said as she adjusted her hard hat. "I've also got a call into the lawyer who defended him and the Assistant District Attorney who prosecuted. Not to mention Tex and my buddy, Mozart, are doing their own brand of digging."

"We got a bullet," Jax called from the bedroom.

"That would be the prick in our asses," Harper said with a smile.

"My mom is going to like you." The words whooshed out of his mouth before his brain had a chance to comprehend how she might take that sentiment. It had been two days, and here he was wanting to take her back home to meet the family.

She arched a brow.

"I just meant that—"

She squeezed his biceps. "Let's get through this case and then maybe," she said, waggling her finger, "we can talk about whatever this is, but I'm not up for meeting your mother any time soon."

"She's coming down in two weeks, so it might be sooner rather than later."

Harper let out an audible gasp.

God, he wanted to yank her in his arms and kiss those pouty lips.

Later. Definitely later.

He followed her into the bedroom, where Jax held up a small, charred bullet in a pair of tweezers before dropping it into an evidence bag. "Looks like a forty-five."

"I know Jonathon owned a couple of guns," Hunter said. "I've seen him at the range more than once."

"I own five guns." Brodie had been a gun nut his entire life. He loved going to the range and hunting. The feel of the metal in his hands was almost as intoxicating as hosing down a blaze burning toward the sky. Not that he ever really wanted to have to put out a fire at this point in his life, but it was what he signed on for. "Being a gun owner doesn't mean anything."

"You're defending Jonathon?" Jax asked with a raised brow.

"Not defending, but I was just accused of something based on only one piece of the puzzle, and it didn't feel very good, so I'm trying to give him the benefit of the doubt."

"You're a better man than me," Hunter said. "I'd be jumping on the judgmental bandwagon."

"Even though I think Jonathon is a dick, I don't want to believe he could murder anyone, especially his own brother, in cold blood." Brodie shivered. His sisters meant the world to him, and no matter how mad he'd gotten at them, or they at him, it only lasted five minutes. Even when Brodie and Madison had burned down half the backyard, his siblings didn't think the worst of him. He didn't want to think the worst of a brother in arms.

"So, where is he?" Jax asked the obvious.

Harper's phone rang. "It's Tex." She tapped the speaker button. "Hey, Tex. I've got you on speaker with Brodie, Jax, Hunter, and my assistant."

"Hey, everyone. I'm going to skip the formalities and get right to the point."

"Works for us," Harper said.

Brodie folded his arms across his chest and cocked his head. If you wanted to find someone, Tex was your man. Best the business had to offer.

"I was able to trace some of the funds from overseas back to two local banks. One was Jonathon's girlfriend."

"Guess Jonathon doesn't deserve the benefit of my doubt," Brodie muttered. His mother had always told him that his trusting soul was his biggest strength.

And his strongest weakness.

"No, I'd say he doesn't," Tex's voice bellowed over the speaker. "And it gets weirder."

"How weird?" Brodie asked.

"An hour ago, the off-shore account transferred ten grand into an LLC. Guess whose name is registered as the LLC?"

"How about you just tell us," Harper said.

"Edwin Gladstone."

"Jesus," Brodie muttered.

"Tex, do you have anything else on Edwin for me?" Harper asked, her tone remaining professional, but tight.

"I'm pinging his phone, and it seems he is on the move, heading toward the interstate, I would guess."

"Thanks, Tex. What about Jonathon?"

"I don't have a whereabouts for him, yet. But don't you worry your pretty little head. I'll find him."

"All right. Can you send me the coordinates? I want to cut him off at the pass so I can buy myself some time to get the necessary paperwork together to haul his sorry ass in."

"Done," Tex said. "Talk soon."

"Hey, Louis, any word from our clerk?" Harper tucked her phone and tablet into her bag.

"I'm texting her now."

"Holy shit," Harper said.

"What now?"

"Tex just texted, and an Archer Battle just got off a plane and passed through customs and guess where he was coming from?" Harper asked, shaking her head, her lips pulling down into a frown.

"The Caribbean," Jax, Hunter, and Brodie all said in unison. Of course, Archer was dead, so it had to be Jonathon. But why the hell was he risking coming back into the States?

"Our clerk had a long chat with the ADA that tried the bank robbery," Louis interjected.

"And what did he have to say?" Brodie asked, his mind churning over all the details, and the picture it painted wasn't pretty. But there were more questions than answers.

"He always believed Archer's brother had Archer hide the money, but he never had any proof. When the case was overturned, the DA's office hired a PI, but

Archer gave him the slip about an hour north of here." Louis rolled his forefinger over his cell. "It was Jonathon that pushed hard to have the case overturned."

"Is the PI still around?" Harper asked, her gaze darting between the phone and Brodie.

"I'm not sure," Louis said.

"I'll get Tex to find him," Harper said with a stained voice. "I need to talk to him and find out exactly what he knows."

"There is more, ma'am," Louis said.

"Keep talking." Brodie liked this kid, and he would bet he'd become a great investigator under the direction of Harper. One of the things Brodie found most intriguing about Harper, and how she handled this case, had been her willingness to use all resources available, never letting her own ego get in the way.

Even the way she handled Edwin in the office hadn't been about ego, but about setting a tone that everyone needed to be a team player.

"It seems someone beat the crap out of Ronda," Louis said. "She was found in a hotel room just twenty minutes ago when she failed to check out. She was just admitted to the hospital. Locals are with her now. Our clerk says she called to get a medical status, and the nurse said Ronda was still unconscious, but stable."

"Fuck." Harper dug her hands into her purse. "Louis, get down there and find out what the hell is going on. If any military personnel are mentioned, you tell the locals this is our case. You get any flack, tell them to call me."

"Yes, ma'am."

Bodie scratched the back of his head. "This seems like quite the elaborate plan. One that was years in the making but fell apart somewhere in the execution."

"Unless all of this was part of the plan," Harper said. "Think about it. The brother gets out of prison and comes for his money, but Jonathon isn't going to part with it."

"All right, but where does the girlfriend fit into all this?" Hunter asked, though Brodie suspected everyone had formed the same opinion on that.

"She's his alibi, right, but she fucked that up, so either he beat her up, or Edwin did," Harper said. "Do we know how close Jonathon and Edwin were?"

Brodie shook his head. "I never saw them together."

"I have," Hunter said. "Only once, recently. I thought it was weird when I saw them at Michael's when I was picking up pizza for the kids. They were nose to nose, having a heated discussion. I honestly didn't think anything of it. Jonathon pissed off a lot of people, and I don't know Edwin from Adam."

"We need to know if there is a bigger connection between Edwin and the Battle brothers. Did they grow up near each other? College? Anything."

"Shit," Brodie muttered. "They both went to Ohio State, didn't they?"

"I know for sure Jonathon did," Hunter said. "He bragged about it nonstop."

"I think I saw that in Edwin's records," Harper said as she dug through her bag and pulled out her phone. "I'll have the clerk check on that."

Brodie leaned against the burned-out countertop. It shifted slightly, so he stood tall and stared into Harper's bourbon eyes. They held the gaze for a long moment. "Let's say that Jonathon did indeed keep the money for his brother and never had any intention of sharing it. So, when Archer was acquitted, it was the perfect time to kill him."

"And to set me up to take a murder rap," Brodie said, swallowing the bile that sucker-punched the back of his throat.

"I think you were collateral damage and an easy mark considering your history with him," Hunter stated the obvious, but it didn't make Brodie feel any better, especially because he had been so effortlessly goaded into the fight by Jonathon.

"We need to focus on the connections with Ronda and Edwin," Harper said. "How do you boys feel about helping me comb through a shit ton of paperwork while I go get what I need to pick up Edwin?"

"I'm in," Hunter said.

"Me too, and I bet Ace will be more than happy to help," Jax added.

"Honestly, I'd rather stick with you." Brodie had no idea if she'd allow it, and he'd respect her decision and help out in whatever capacity she needed.

"I'm good with that," she said. "But we'll need to start in my office."

Brodie nodded. He'd taken the arson detail because he liked solving things. He sure as shit was going to like doing it more with Harper.

CHAPTER 13

Brodie went to unlock his front door when he noticed a slight split in the wood. He gently pushed the door, and it popped open an inch.

"Declan, we've got a problem," he said, glancing over his shoulder. Declan was still at the truck, retrieving their breakfast they had purchased from their favorite diner on the way home from the base after a grueling twenty-four shift. Between working Jonathon's arson case and two three-alarm calls in the middle of the night, Brodie wasn't in the mood for more drama.

"What's up?"

Quietly, Brodie made his way across the front path toward his vehicle. "Front door is open, and it looks like it was damaged."

"Damaged how?"

"Kicked in," Brodie said as he reached into the glove box, finding his pistol. The neighborhood had its share of break-ins. Usually kids walking by, seeing someone's purse or a wallet by the door. But most of the crimes were things stolen from cars and the occasional domestic dispute.

"Shit." Declan tossed the take-out boxes on top of the cargo bed cover before snagging his overnight bag, which was where he carried his weapon. Neither one ever left home without one. "I'll take the back."

"Meet me in the middle," Brodie said. Their rental had two entrances. One off the back patio near the kitchen and the front door with a small foyer next to the family room. They'd scan the main living areas before the bedrooms. Brodie doubted anyone was still inside, but better safe than sorry.

With his gun at the ready, he pushed back the door, scanning the room. He noted nothing out of place. Out of the corner of his eye, he saw Declan down the hallway in the kitchen.

Declan raised his hand under his neck, waving it back and forth, giving the 'nothing' signal.

Together, they made their way down the hallway

toward the bedrooms. The first one on the right was Brodie's room.

"Shit," he said. "Look." He pointed to his dresser. Two drawers were hanging open, clothes haphazardly dangling out. Everyone teased Brodie about his obsessive neatness. Nothing out of place and his bed was always perfectly made.

This time, not so much. Brodie hadn't slept in it since he met Harper, and he knew he'd left the corners tucked neatly like his mother had taught him, not falling out under the comforter.

"Let me check my room," Declan said as he stepped by and pushed open the second door on the right. "Nothing touched in here."

Brodie turned, staring at the open door of the third bedroom that they used as a shared office of sorts. "We always keep that door closed."

"I shut it when we left yesterday morning," Declan whispered.

"I haven't been in that room in three days." Brodie raised his weapon.

"Yeah, you haven't been home since the pretty investigator moved in across the street. I'm starting to feel like you don't love me anymore."

"I don't," Brodie teased, but his voice was strained with worry.

He sucked in a breath, pointing his weapon into the room as he stepped across the threshold and made a quick scan.

No one was in there, but his gun cabinet, which he always kept locked, had been damaged and someone managed to open it.

"Two of my guns are gone."

"That's not good," Declan said, holstering his weapon.

"Worse, your guns are untouched," Brodie said, pointing to a similar cabinet with the lock still firmly in place.

"Fuck," Declan muttered.

"I have a bad feeling about this." Ever since Brodie left the base an hour ago, he felt like he had to keep glancing over his shoulder, waiting for Edwin or Jonathon to appear out of nowhere. He certainly didn't like the fact that Harper had spent the night alone. If the two men were in cahoots, she could be in danger, regardless of her independence and her tough exterior. He had texted her throughout the night while on base and she at home. Most times, she responded within minutes, since she said she'd be up late working, but those wee hours of the morning, where he knew she was sound asleep, drove him crazy with worry.

"I'll call the locals, and you can call your girlfriend."

"Let's call Harper first. She may not want the locals involved."

"Dude, your guns were stolen, we need to report that," Declan said, glaring at him.

"Give me two minutes." He whipped out his phone. "Hey, Siri, call Harper D."

"Harper D?" Declan questioned with a quiet laugh.

Brodie shrugged. "I was lazy, and I like the sound of it."

"Hey, Brodie." The sound of Harper's voice sliced through the tension, easing his tight neck muscles. "Are you home?"

"Just pulled in," he admitted. "But I've got a problem."

"What kind of problem?" she asked.

"My house was broken into sometime in the last twenty-four hours, and two of my guns are missing. One is an older Marlon 795 that my dad bought me years ago, and the other is a Ruger semi-automatic."

"Fuck, that's not good. Have you called it in?" she asked.

"No. I wanted to talk with you first. I don't believe in coincidences, and my gut is telling me this is related to Jonathon and Edwin." Brodie turned and stepped out of the office. He didn't want to disturb anything more than he already had.

"Did Jonathon know about your gun collection?" Harper asked.

"Oh yeah. He used to want to brag about how his collection was the best around. Hell, that night we got into a fight, he wanted me to show him mine."

"Did you?" Harper asked.

"I don't do pissing contests. I told him to fuck off. He went into the house and about fifteen minutes later, he came out with a beer and started in on Becca." Brodie followed Declan out of the house and back toward the driveway, where he leaned against the hood of his truck.

"That's when you asked him to leave."

"Yep. He didn't, and I did a dumb thing," Brodie said. "Do you want me to call the locals?"

"I'll send Louis over. Once he gets there, yes, call it in."

"All right." In the background, he heard the sound of a horn. "Where are you?"

"In the car heading to a lead."

"What kind of lead?" he asked.

"I'll let you know if it pans out. I gotta go."

"Hey, Harper?" His chest tightened like it did the

first time he'd heard about a fire that his sister had been called to and two firefighters had been injured. He'd been home on leave, and he and his mom paced in the living room until the dreaded call came in.

His sister had indeed been injured, though not badly, but still, that feeling had unsettled him in a way he prayed he never had to deal with again.

"Yeah?" she responded softly.

"Be safe out there and text me every once in a while."

"I will, you do the same."

He wanted to say something sweet and romantic, but he wouldn't do that in front of Declan. Not while the man had a shit-eating grin on his face.

"Bye," Brodie said as he tapped the off button. "Louis is on the way over, then we'll call the locals."

"Damn, man, you're falling faster and harder than Jax did for Scarlet."

"That's impossible." Only Brodie knew, his heart would never belong to anyone but Harper.

The last thing Harper needed was Brodie freaking

out on her, which is why she opted not to tell him where she was going or what she was doing.

She flashed her badge to a local sheriff as she entered the motel room in one of the shadier sides of town. It smelled like a combination of mold and urine. A detective stood at the end of the bed. He wore a dark-blue sport coat, and his badge hung around his neck. He waved her over.

"You must be Major Dawson," the man said.

"Call me Harper."

"Okay, you can call me Cash."

Harper covered her mouth and stared down at the lifeless body sprawled out on a yellow-white comforter that looked like it might not have been washed for months.

"That's definitely Edwin Gladstone." She planted her hands on her hips and scanned the room. A few papers scattered across the floor near the desk which had been pushed up under a window that had a thick layer of soot, making it difficult to see out of. Gladstone had just been given ten grand. Why the hell was he staying in a two-star motel that often rented by the hour to prostitutes?

"Tell me what you know," she said, releasing a long breath. Three days on the job and she had two dead bodies, a woman who had been beaten nearly to death, and two soldiers that had gone AWOL.

"The desk clerk said this man checked in late last night. According to the clerk, the victim appeared nervous and agitated. At about seven this morning, the same clerk saw a dark pickup truck pull up in front of the unit, and a man got out and knocked on the door." Cash turned, nodding toward the entrance. "Then the clerk said he started to prepare for shift change and went into the back room. That's when he thought he heard rapid gunfire."

"Rapid, as in an assault rifle?" She examined the walls, the bed, and the body for bullet wounds.

"No, more like semi, but that's not what the clerk said. He described it as seven or so pow, pow, pows. As if there was a break in between."

"So, maybe a semi," she said more to herself.

"I'll get to the weapon in a second." Cash planted his hands on his hips. "The clerk said he fell to the ground, not knowing how far away the shots were. He said about a ten-minute silence followed, but he was too scared to move until he heard the truck leave."

"How'd he know it was the truck?" she asked.

"That's where it gets weird. When asked, he gave a decent answer, as in, he didn't know until he went back to the office and called the police. But the prostitute and her john in the room next door said they never saw a pickup, and after the gunshots, which they described the same way, they looked out the window and saw a nondescript four-door sedan peel out of the parking lot."

"I take it you questioned the clerk again," she said as a statement not a question.

"My partner did, while I took a look around the lobby. But while standing behind the clerk, I saw two fresh one-hundred-dollar bills in his back pocket. He's amended his story, now saying he was paid by some man, medium to tall build, with blue eyes and dark hair to tell us he saw a pickup."

Harper's heart thumped to her throat. "Before or after the shots were fired?"

"Before," Cash said.

"Where is the clerk now?" Harper struggled to keep her hands from trembling.

Cash pointed to the door again. "In the office. My partner is with him, making sure he doesn't leave."

"I want to question him, but before I do that, you said something about getting to the murder weapon in a minute."

"We found a Ruger semi-automatic in the dumpster."

She cocked her head while her pulse raced out of control. She knew Jonathon was behind this and wanted desperately to pin it on Brodie. But why? "What made you look in the dumpster?"

"The clerk said he saw the man who paid him toss something in there."

"I need to talk to this clerk." She followed Cash out of the motel room and across the parking lot with grass and wild weeds growing up through major cracks in the pavement. Inside the musty lobby was one of those fish things that sings an Elvis tune whenever anyone walks by hanging over a sofa across from the lobby desk. A scrawny young man, maybe in his mid-twenties, sat on the sofa. Thankfully the fish didn't sing when she stepped in front of him.

She pulled out her phone, bringing up an image of Jonathon and held it out. "Is this the man who paid you to give the police false information? The man that walked into that room and shot and killed someone?"

"I didn't see no one get shot," the clerk said with a shaky voice.

"Did the man have a rifle in his hands when he entered the room?"

The clerk nodded.

"Then you heard gunshots."

The clerk nodded again.

She pushed the phone closer. "Is this the man?"

"Yes. That's him."

"Thank you," she said, showing the image to Cash. "This is Senior Firefighter Jonathon Battle. He's gone AWOL. I'm putting out an official statement and would appreciate your cooperation."

"I'll put out an APB now," Cash said with a frown. "It's hard when one of our own turns on us. You can count on my department to assist in any way."

"Thanks. If you don't mind, I'm going to send my forensics team out here. We can split the workload based on which one of us will get faster results."

"Works for me."

"Do you mind staying here and seeing this through? I need to go warn the soldier that Jonathon is trying to set up. I think he'll go after him next."

"It will be my pleasure."

She shook Cash's hand and made a beeline for her car. "Hey, Siri, call Brodie Welch."

The phone went straight to voicemail.

"Fuck," she muttered as she punched the gas. "Hey, Siri, call Brodie Welch."

Same thing.

"Hey, Siri, text Brodie Welch. Where are you?"

Her heart raced as she sped through the streets. She gripped the steering wheel so tight her knuckles turned white.

Five minutes passed and finally a response.

"Hey, Siri, read my texts."

"You have one new text from Brodie Welch. I'm at your house."

"Thank God. Hey, Siri, send a text to Brodie Welch. I'm on my way."

CHAPTER 14

Brodie twisted the key to the front door of Harper's house. When he left the base, she'd given him a set of keys, so he could get in and fix a leaky faucet. Since he knew he wouldn't be able to sleep well, he figured he'd do that before even trying to take a much-needed snooze.

The lock stuck slightly, and the door squeaked as he pushed it open. Another thing he could tinker with to occupy his time, and mind.

He closed the door and stepped into the family room. A breeze tickled the back of his neck, and he turned toward the hallway.

"What the—"

The crack of metal smashing into the side of his head sent a sharp pain from one temple to the other.

It was as if someone pushed a cold knife through his head and yanked it back out. He reached for the wall, blinking, trying to focus, but everything blurred.

His knees hit the floor with a loud thud. Seconds later, another sharp pain vibrated through his skull, and the world faded to black.

Harper slammed the gear shift into park before yanking the keys from the ignition and bolting to her front door.

Without thinking, she twisted the knob and raced inside, skidding to a stop in the middle of the hallway.

"Brodie," she whispered, staring at his body slumped over on a chair in the middle of the living room. His hands were behind his back, and his ankles were taped to the wooden legs. His head flopped forward, and a trace of blood trickled down the side of his cheek. The smell of gasoline lingered in the air.

"You got here quickly," a male voice said from behind her.

She turned on her heels and gasped. Jonathon

leaned against the wall between the dining room and the foyer with a lighter in one hand and a gun in the other.

"This isn't going to end well for you," she said, balling her fists. She should have listened to that tiny voice in her head that told her something wasn't quite right when she pulled into her driveway.

"That's where you're wrong." He rolled his finger over the silver wheel of the lighter. A tall flame flashed in front of his face. "You might have put a few pieces of the puzzle together, but at the end of the day, the world is going to think Brodie over there lost his mind. He killed Edwin—"

"That little set-up has been thwarted. The clerk sung like a canary and ID'd you. Besides, Brodie had been reinstated, so he was either on base at the station, or at a call."

Brodie groaned in the background.

Jonathon's smile faded a tad, and she could tell his mind was churning over what that meant for his current situation. "Looks like I've underestimated you," he said, still flicking that damn, stupid lighter. "But at the end of the day, it's not going to matter. He'll be dead. You'll be dead. And I'll be gone, because you know I'm dead."

"Everyone knows it was your brother who died

in that fire, which you set. Give it up, Jonathon, you're fucked."

He shrugged his shoulders. "Maybe I'll end up a fugitive, but you've got to love countries that have no extradition laws, and I've got the cash to get me a private jet to take me there."

"You still have to go through customs and Archer Battle won't make it through any security checkpoint as a wanted man."

"Now you underestimate me," Jonathon said, inching closer. "Do you know how many millions my brother heisted from that bank?"

Another audible moan by Brodie.

As Jonathon inched forward, she took a few baby steps backward, toward Brodie.

"All marked bills."

"Not anymore. Well, all but five hundred thousand." Jonathon pointed to a large bag. "Which will be strategically placed across the street where the authorities will find it. They will either think Brodie, and maybe that idiot Declan, took a deal from me, or they will think they had something to do with my disappearance. There are enough unanswered questions and very little substantial evidence to prove that I was involved in anything."

Wow. Jonathon was more delusional than Edwin

had been. The things she and her team had uncovered would not only prove Jonathon committed murder, but it would get him sent to Gitmo. She decided there was no point in arguing with him. He believed he'd walk out of here unscathed. Who was she to try to burst that bubble. Of course, she'd enjoy the fuck out of it when she slapped handcuffs on that sorry piece of shit.

"So, let me guess. You found a way to launder the money through an LLC in an off-shore account."

"Oh, look at you, all full of yourself because you think you're so smart. Doesn't take a detective to figure that one out, but hey, I'll pat your backside and stroke your pretty little ego so you can feel good about yourself."

She gritted her teeth, making a growling noise. His sarcasm made her want to spit in his face, after she broke his nose with a quick jab.

Brodie grunted.

Two grunts.

And then a moan.

She let out a long sigh.

Brodie did too.

Hot damn, he was awake. While that didn't change the situation much, it made her feel better.

Hopefully, Jonathon hadn't caught on to that little game.

"Since we're on the subject, let me see if I have all this straight."

Jonathon glanced at his watch. "You've got ten minutes. Then you can kiss your dick boyfriend goodbye."

She'd make good use of the time while she figured out how to take Jonathon down.

"You helped your brother get out of prison just so he could be your dead body double." She moved even closer to Brodie, standing about two paces away and directly in front of him. Planting her hands on her hips, she lifted the back of her shirt, just so Brodie could see her weapon. Jonathon's biggest mistake hadn't been underestimating her but overestimating himself.

Now, she just needed a plan. One that Brodie would understand through osmosis or some such shit.

"You're really going to bore me with this crap," Jonathon said as he moved his leg behind the wall in the foyer before kicking a gas can into view. "Just so you know, I've doused—"

"I can smell it. Can we get to the details? There

are a few things my tiny little brain hasn't been able to wrap my head around."

Jonathon laughed. "You're a feisty lady. I bet you're a good fuck."

She waggled her finger behind her back, hoping Brodie could actually see it and understand that he should do nothing, even though he was the kind of man that was fiercely protective of what he might consider his. But it was more than that with Brodie. His sense of honor and duty pulled him to protect, no matter the cost to himself.

He proved that the day he nearly died saving the General's life.

Jonathon leaned to the side. "Shocked that didn't rouse the poor bastard, but I did clock him good, and he is a pussy."

"My time is running out, and I really have a few more questions."

"Fine." Jonathon shoved the gas can toward her feet. "While you talk, I want you to pour that around the sofa. Feel free to douse some on yourself as well as Brodie."

Like hell.

"Why beat the crap out of your girlfriend?" Harper asked.

"She wasn't really my girlfriend. Just a means to

an end. At the time, the investigation was still looking like Brodie would be blamed for everything. Actually, if you hadn't shown up, he would have. Kudos to you for thwarting that."

If she wasn't so disgusted by the man standing in front of her, she might have been flattered. "What about Edwin? Didn't you need him on the inside?"

"Again, you showed up. But when he went AWOL, I had to kill him, and since he accused Brodie a little too quickly, I thought it might lead the investigation back to Brodie if I made it look as if he could have done it."

"So, you stole his guns," she said matter-of-factly.

"Such a smart girl."

His sarcasm wasn't lost on her. "Why give Edwin money?" She bent over, careful not to reveal her weapon and picked up the gas can, using it as an excuse to get closer to Brodie.

"So he'd think I was coming back to help him get out of the country."

"You took a big risk coming back."

"Perhaps, but I really want Brodie dead."

She swallowed. "Why? What did he ever do to you?" This was the one piece of the puzzle she hadn't been able to figure out. Other than basic male ego, she'd seen nothing substantial regarding their history to lead her to believe Brodie had done anything so horrible that even Jonathon would hold a grudge.

Jonathon's face contorted as if someone stabbed him in the heart. His lips pursed, and his eyes narrowed into tiny slits shooting daggers in her direction.

"Brodie and I aren't much different. We both love fires and have an odd thrill for setting them. He says he doesn't, but you should see him when he sets a bonfire. It's like he's an artist standing in front of a blank canvas waiting for the first stroke of the paintbrush."

Something touched the back of her foot. She stood very still, hoping it wasn't a cockroach, but instead Brodie.

"That still doesn't explain why you want him dead."

"I wish he was awake to hear this, because I'd love to see the look in his eyes when I tell him what he prevented me from doing." Jonathon wiped the perspiration beading across forehead. "You see, when he was seventeen, he happened to be at the same ski lodge my family went to. I had just found out my mother had been having an affair with the General, who was there with his wife and kids. Imagine that. My mother and the General, sneaking off to fuck in the snow somewhere."

"Shit, you started the fire at the Cambridge Ski Lodge?" In one thought, everything snapped into place. She remembered reading in Jonathon's records that his parents divorced a year after he enlisted.

"I wanted the General to burn. I had locked him in the bathroom and then stood back and watched that lodge go up in smoke. What a fucking hard-on that gave me. But then the fake do-gooder goes and runs in and saves the day. Asshole."

Chills ran up her body, coating her skin like snow falling from the sky. "Your mother died in a house fire."

"Jesus," Brodie muttered from behind her. "You're a fucking piece of work."

"I wondered if you were faking."

"Fake this, you dirt bag." Brodie snagged the gun from her holster and shoved her to the floor.

Two shots rang out as heat erupted all around her.

"Get out," Brodie yelled.

She stood, jumping over a flame as her house quickly turned into a fireball, and thick, black smoke bellowed to the ceiling. She covered her mouth, blinking wildly through the smolder.

"You bastard." Brodie swung, his fist landing square on Jonathon's jaw.

Jonathon laughed as he wiped the blood from his face, rushing forward and crashing into Brodie. Flames flickered around their bodies as they rolled on the floor. She took a pillow and swatted at Brodie's pant leg, which had caught fire.

"If you can, get the guns. But if not, just get out and get help." Brodie shifted his body, but Jonathon had him pinned.

"Harper. Now!" Brodie yelled.

She stood there for a second, blinking. The heat filling the room, choking her more than the smoke. The sound of fabric catching fire filled her ears. The smell of burning flesh tickled her nose as she looked down at her burning arm. Quickly, she took the same pillow and smothered the flames. She found both guns and ran from the house, screaming and searching her back pocket for her cell, which was nowhere to be found. Once across the street, she started banging on Declan's door.

"What the hell is going... fuck." Declan held her by the hands. "Is Brodie in there?"

She nodded. “Jonathon too. I must have dropped my phone.”

“Use the landline.” Declan took off running.

“Where are you going?”

“I’m a fireman, where the hell do you think I’m going?”

Brodie did his best to ignore the intense heat as he struggled to get the upper hand. The fire raged around them, and the gas stung his eyes. His ankles were still taped to the sides of the chair legs, though the chair had since shattered to pieces. Brodie managed to pin Jonathon down. He sat on Jonathon’s stomach and held his arms over his head.

The flames roared to the ceiling and sparks flew, snapping at his already burned body. He had to get out, and soon, or they’d both perish.

“I’m letting you go,” he said, easing up on Jonathon’s arms. “You’re not worth dying for.” Brodie jumped to his feet.

“You shouldn’t have let me go. Now I’m going to kill you.” Jonathon slowly stood, an evil smile spreading across his face.

“Come on, you can kill me outside.” Brodie

turned and smiled when he saw Declan race through the front door.

"I wouldn't do that if I were you," Declan said as he stepped over some of the flames, holding a shotgun. "You can come out with us, or you can burn. The choice is yours."

Brodie glanced over his shoulder as Jonathon tried to run for the back door.

Bang!

Jonathon screamed as he hit the floor, holding his knee.

Declan pointed to Brodie's arms and side. "You're burned pretty bad. Get out of here. I'll handle Jonathon."

Brodie nodded as he stepped through the front door, keeping an eye on Declan, who dragged Jonathon out by his arms.

"Brodie!" Harper's voice filled his heart with joy.

He turned and hobbled toward the street. The sound of fire engines echoed in the background. People came out of their houses, asking how they could help, but all Brodie could focus on was putting his arms around Harper.

"Sorry about the house. It's not going to be livable for a while, but you can stay with me." He kissed her forehead, but she took a step back.

"What? Too soon to ask you to move in?"

"Those burns are bad. Really bad."

As the adrenaline wore off, scorching pain hit his mind with the force of a volcano. His knees buckled.

"Lie down," Harper whispered.

"Here, in the middle of the street? That's stupid." But he could no longer hold his own weight. He rested his head in her lap and closed his eyes. People shouted around him. The ground shook as fireman raced past.

"Leave it to one of my men to play hero."

He could have sworn that was Ace's voice, but he couldn't open his eyes to make sure. All he wanted to do was picture his happy place, which was in Harper's arms. With her, he could do anything, including ignoring the pain.

Someone put something on his body that made him scream like a dying pig. Or at least he thought he had screamed.

He twitched as a needle pricked his arm. Fluid immediately filled his veins and oh, it carried with it a cocktail of I-will-no-longer-give-a-shit painkillers.

His breathing slowed, and he tried to just enjoy the medical high and Harper's soft hands in his hair.

"I've seen worse."

This time it was Hunter's voice that filled his ears.

"You're an ugly asshole," Brodie said, blinking his eyes open.

"I love you too," Hunter said with a laugh.

"I think that's Harper's line." Brodie shifted his gaze.

Harper smiled.

That was all he needed.

"I've fallen hard for you, Major Harper Dawson."

"You're in pain and doped up on drugs." She bent over and kissed his forehead. "But I've fallen even harder for you, Captain Crew Chief Brodie Welch."

EPILOGUE

Six months later…

"You didn't tell me your fiancé was a toddler whisperer."

Harper laughed at Mozart's comment as she watched Brodie play in the kiddie pool with April, Mozart's daughter, who had just turned three and was growing so fast.

"I'd say he's a keeper," Summer, Mozart's wife, said. She pushed back the lounge chair and rested her feet on Mozart's lap. "Can we get a Brodie? I could use a full-time Brodie."

"What's wrong with a full-time me?" Mozart teased.

"That's the point, honey. Having him around would give us more alone time together."

"Alone time is what got us April in the first place," Mozart said with a big smile. "I'm not opposed to another one of those."

"Get a room." Harper stared at Brodie. The scars from his burns were healing nicely, though he'd need another surgery after the wedding.

Marriage.

She couldn't believe how quickly her life had changed. For the better. "You should see him around his sister's kids. They all think he's the best thing since sliced bread."

"He's pretty damn close," Mozart said. "The General told me how that man saved his life."

"Brodie plays it down. He plays everything he's ever done down, like it's just another day."

"It is for him, you know that," Mozart said.

She nodded. She understood that Brodie, or men like him and Mozart, didn't like to wear their jobs on their sleeves. They chose their careers because they couldn't imagine doing anything else. It wasn't an obligation.

It was a way of life.

One she accepted.

Her eyes welled with tears. "He doesn't even

remember that when he came out of that house, his body was on fire."

"You need to stop dwelling on that." Mozart patted her knee.

"I almost said no to his proposal," she admitted.

"Well, don't tell him I told you this, but he called when you asked if you could think about it," Mozart said as he blew a kiss to his little girl, who blew one back, then started begging Brodie to do the same.

"He looked so heartbroken, but the whole things scares me. Everyone I've ever loved has—"

"You really need to knock that off," Mozart said with a fatherly tone. "Because I love you, and I don't plan on going anywhere."

"Me too," Summer said, poking Harper in the side with her big toe. "April loves you even more."

"I know. That's why I said yes two hours later. I've been trying to make it up to him ever since."

"I'm sure he understands," Summer said. She always had a way of making Harper feel better about anything and everything.

"Daddy!" April yelled as she ran across the grass. "Why can't I marry Brodie?" she asked with big tears rolling down her cheeks.

"I didn't handle that one too well, now did I?" Brodie tapped Harper on the shoulder, motioning for her to inch forward. He straddled the lounge chair and eased in behind her, pulling her back to his chest.

Mozart kissed April's forehead as he smoothed down her hair. "Same reason you can't marry Daddy."

"Oh," April said, her little lip quivering.

"Now, I know how to deal with that question, if it every happens again," Brodie said, holding up his bottle of beer. "Did you ask him yet?"

"No," Harper said, glancing over her shoulder, giving him the evil eye. She didn't know why she struggled with this question, but she worried it would be awkward for Mozart. Or his family.

"Ask me what?" Mozart asked.

"Well, for starters, we were hoping you'd let April be the flower girl in our wedding." Harper took Brodie's beer, but then thought better of it and handed it back. He gave her an odd look, but then shrugged and went back to sipping the brew.

"You've set a date?" Summer asked, her feet hitting the ground as she sat up straight.

"You didn't tell them that either?" Brodie massaged her neck with his long fingers. "Well, I've give you some slack since we just decided a few days ago."

"Awe, thanks honey," she said not hiding her sarcasm.

He kissed her nose playfully.

"Don't leave us hanging. When is the big day?" Mozart asked.

"This Saturday, May 2nd, at eleven in the morning, on the beach, just family," Harper said, choking on the sob that threatened to escape. Brodie had been so wonderful about the date and time, and even now, he told her if she ever changed her mind, even the day of the wedding, he'd understand. But she wanted to make her sister's death and her father's suicide mean something special. She wanted to change the dread of that day, into the promise of something wonderful.

Something forever.

Mozart cleared this throat. "I think that's the perfect day for the joyous event. Lucky for you we planned on staying for the weekend."

Brodie nudged her in the back.

"Mozart?" she started, her voice thick with emotion. "I was hoping...we were hoping ...you'd give me away." She bit down on her lower lip. Tears, not unlike April's, dotted her cheeks. Damn hormones.

His hand ran up and down his daughter's back.

His eyes glazed over as the corners of his mouth turned upward. "I'd be honored."

"Thank you," she said softly as she wiped the tears away. "And Summer, I'd be thrilled if you'd be the maid of honor."

"Absolutely," Summer said. "Anything for you. So, what handsome fireman do I get to walk the beach aisle with?

Harper groaned. "We need to talk my future husband out of this one."

"Hell no," Brodie said. "You picked just about everything. I get this one thing."

"What's wrong with the best man?" Summer asked.

"Nothing. My twin sister is amazing, and we made a promise to each other years ago to stand up for each other."

Mozart broke out laughing so badly he started coughing.

"It's not that funny," Brodie said with a scowl. "She's my best friend. We've been through a lot together."

"It's not that, son," Mozart said. "I'm all about family, but what happens when she gets married? I mean, I'm trying really hard not to picture you in a pink taffeta bridesmaid dress."

"Oh my God. That's quite the visual," Harper said, covering her mouth.

"I guess I hadn't thought that one through." Brodie took another beer from the cooler. "But you can't talk me out of this one. It's one of those weird twin things."

"Do twins run in the family?" Summer asked.

"They do. Mostly paternal, but I do have one set of cousins that are identical."

The idea of one baby was enough to make Harper run for the hills, but two? What the hell had she gotten herself into?

"So, there is a good chance you guys could have twins, then." Summer's wide smile was all-knowing.

"I suppose, but we're a long way from that happening." Brodie took another swig of his beer.

"Not to be rude, but your bride to be is—"

"Summer, can I get you a drink?"

"No, honey, and it's never a good idea to avoid or keep things from your husband. Take it from someone who's been married for a bit."

"Oh my. Really? You're—"

"Don't say it," Harper said, interrupting Mozart. The cat was halfway out of the bag, but she had to be the one to blurt out the words.

"I'm seriously lost on this conversation," Brodie said.

She turned in the chair so they could be face to face. "I've been trying to find the right time and right words to tell you this for the last two days, but we've had company, and now the wedding, and honestly, I have no idea how you're going to take the news."

"You really enjoy freaking me out, don't you?"

"It's not intentional but yeah, I do."

"She also likes avoiding things," Mozart said.

"That too, but I can't avoid this." She took his hand and placed it over her belly.

Brodie glanced down, then back up.

He repeated the head nod five times as the knowledge of what it meant slowly made its way to his brain. His eyes went wide. "No way," he said. His fingers gently dug into her muscles. "You can't be. We always use... oh, wait, we didn't that one time."

"Children in the house," Mozart said, laughing as he set April down. She'd become bored with the adult conversation and waddled back to the baby pool where she climbed in to play with her barbies.

"One time is all it takes to make a baby, but in your case, it might have made two," Summer said as she stood, holding her hand out to Mozart. "Let's give the two lovebirds a minute alone."

"Yes, dear."

Harper waited until Mozart and Summer settled in the grass near their daughter. "You okay? I know this wasn't planned and probably way too soon, but—"

Brodie pressed his index finger against her lips. "The best things in life are unexpected. Like falling in love with you and this." He patted her stomach. "I love everything about you, Harper, and I can't wait to start a family with you."

The End

More Books by Jen Talty

ABOUT THE AUTHOR

Jen Talty is an award-winning author of Romantic Suspense. Dark Water hit #10 in Barnes and Noble and her books have been in the top 50 on Amazon. Jennifer grew up in Rochester, New York. She recently retired from being a full-time hockey mom as her children hung up their skates. She and her husband still live in Rochester while her children travel globe. Jen was the co-founder of Cool Gus Publishing with NY Times Bestselling Author Bob Mayer.

Sign up for Jen's Newsletter where she often gives away free books before publication.
Join Jen's private Facebook group where she posts exclusive excerpts and discuss all things murder and love!

ALSO BY JEN TALTY

The New York State Trooper Series

In Two Weeks

Dark Water

Deadly Secrets

Murder in Paradise Bay

To Protect His Own

Deadly Seduction

When a Stranger Calls

Federal Investigator Series

Jane Doe's Return

The Butterfly Murders

THE MEN OF THEIF LAKE

Rekindled

THE OMEGA TEAM: THE SARICH BROTHERS

The Lighthouse

Her Last Hope

The Last Flight

Coming Soon:

The Return Home

The Phoenix Agency: The Raven Sisters

The Lost Sister

The Lost Solider

Coming Soon:

The Lost Soul

The Lost Connection

SPECIAL FORCES: FIRE PROTECTION SPECIALISTS

Burning Desire

Burning Kiss

Burning Skies

Burning Lies

Coming soon:

Burning Heart

Burning Bed

Burning Oath

Burning River

The Brotherhood Protectors: Out Of The Wild

Rough Justice

Coming Soon:

Rough Around the Edges

Rough Ride

As you know, this book included at least one character from Susan Stoker's books. To check out more, see below.

Delta Force Heroes Series

Rescuing Rayne (FREE!)

Rescuing Aimee

Rescuing Emily

Rescuing Harley

Marrying Emily

Rescuing Kassie

Rescuing Bryn

Rescuing Casey

Rescuing Sadie

Rescuing Wendy

Rescuing Mary (Oct 2018)

Rescuing Macie (April 2019)

Badge of Honor: Texas Heroes Series

Justice for Mackenzie (FREE!)

Justice for Mickie

Justice for Corrie

Justice for Laine (novella)

Shelter for Elizabeth

Justice for Boone

Shelter for Adeline

Shelter for Sophie

Justice for Erin

Justice for Milena

Shelter for Blythe

Justice for Hope (Sept 2018)

Shelter for Quinn (TBA)

Shelter for Koren (TBA)

Shelter for Penelope (TBA)

SEAL of Protection Series

Protecting Caroline (FREE!)

Protecting Alabama

Protecting Fiona

Marrying Caroline (novella)

Protecting Summer

Protecting Cheyenne

Protecting Jessyka

Protecting Julie (novella)

Protecting Melody

Protecting the Future

Protecting Alabama's Kids (novella)

Protecting Kiera (novella)

Protecting Dakota

New York Times, *USA Today* and *Wall Street Journal*

Bestselling Author Susan Stoker has a heart as big as the state of Texas where she lives, but this all American girl has also spent the last fourteen years living in Missouri, California, Colorado, and Indiana. She's married to a retired Army man who now gets to follow *her* around the country.

She debuted her first series in 2014 and quickly followed that up with the SEAL of Protection Series, which solidified her love of writing and creating stories readers can get lost in.

If you enjoyed this book, or any book, please consider leaving a review. It's appreciated by authors more than you'll know.

www.stokeraces.com
susan@stokeraces.com

More Books in the Special Forces: Operation Alpha World!

Brynne Asher - Blackburn

Denise Agnew - Dangerous to Hold

Shauna Allen: Awakening Aubrey

Shauna Allen: Defending Danielle

Shauna Allen: Rescuing Rebekah

Shauna Allen: Saving Scarlett

Shauna Allen: Saving Grace

Jillian Anselmi: Protecting Ava

Jennifer Becker: Hiding Catherine

Julia Bright: Saving Lorelei

Victoria Bright: Surviving Savage

Victoria Bright: Jostling Joker

Victoria Bright: Going Ghost

Kendra Mei Chailyn: Beast

Kendra Mei Chailyn: Barbie

Kendra Mei Chailyn: Pitbull

Melissa Kay Clarke: Rescuing Annabeth

Samantha A. Cole: Handling Haven

Samantha A. Cole: Cheating the Devil

Sue Coletta: Hacked

KaLyn Cooper: Rescuing Melina

Liz Crowe: Marking Mariah

Jordan Dane: Redemption for Avery

Jordan Dane: Fiona's Salvation

Delilah Devlin: Between a SEAL & A Hard Place

Delilah Devlin: Headover SEAL

Riley Edwards: Protecting Olivia

Riley Edwards: Redeeming Violet

Nicole Flockton: Protecting Maria

Nicole Flockton: Guarding Erin

Nicole Flockton: Guarding Suzie

Nicole Flockton: Guarding Brielle

Fifi Flowers: Protecting Maya

Fifi Flowers: Shielding Alice

Casey Hagen: Shielding Nebraska

Casey Hagen: Shielding Harlow

Casey Hagen: Shielding Josie

Desiree Holt: Protecting Maddie

Kathy Ivan: Saving Sarah

Kathy Ivan: Saving Savannah

Kathy Ivan: Saving Stephanie

Jesse Jacobson: Protecting Honor

Jesse Jacobson: Fighting for Honor

Jesse Jacobson: Defending Honor

Jesse Jacobson: Summer Breeze

Silver James: Rescue Moon

Silver James: SEAL Moon

Silver James: Assassin's Moon

Becca Jameson: Saving Sofia

Heather Long: Securing Arizona

Heather Long: Guarding Gertrude

Heather Long: Protecting Pilar

Heather Long: Covering Coco

Kirsten Lynn: Joining Forces for Jesse

Margaret Madigan: Bang for the Buck

Margaret Madigan: Buck the System

Margaret Madigan: Jungle Buck

Margaret Madigan: December Chill

Rachel McNeely: The SEAL's Surprise Baby

Rachel McNeely: The SEAL's Surprise Bride

KD Michaels: Saving Laura

KD Michaels: Protecting Shane

Wren Michaels: Shadow of Doubt

Wren Michaels: The Fox & The Hound

Wren Michaels: Kisses from the Kremlin

Wren Michaels: Shadow of Doubt

Kat Mizera: Protecting Bobbi

LeTeisha Newton: Protecting Butterfly

LeTeisha Newton: Protecting Goddess

LeTeisha Newton: Protecting Vixen

LeTeisha Newton: Protecting Heartbeat

MJ Nightingale: Protecting Beauty

MJ Nightingale: Betting on Benny

MJ Nightingale: Protecting Secrets

Sarah O'Rourke: Saving Liberty

Debra Parmley: Protecting Pippa

Caleb Pirtle: Lovely Night to Die

Lainey Reese: Protecting New York

Jenika Snow: Protecting Lily

Lynne St James: Protecting Faith

Lynne St James: Protecting Ariana

Jen Talty: Burning Desire

Jen Talty: Burning Kiss

Jen Talty: Burning Skies

Jen Talty: Burning Lies

Megan Vernon: Protecting Us

Megan Vernon: Protecting Earth

Made in the USA
Monee, IL
18 February 2020

21989570R00120